YOU MAY SEE A STRANGER

YOU MAY SEE A STRANGER

STORIES

Paula Whyman

TRIQUARTERLY BOOKS

NORTHWESTERN UNIVERSITY PRESS

EVANSTON, ILLINOIS

TriQuarterly Books
Northwestern University Press
www.nupress.northwestern.edu

Printed in the United States of America

10   9   8   7   6   5   4   3   2   1

Library of Congress Cataloging-in-Publication Data

Names: Whyman, Paula, author.
Title: You may see a stranger : stories / Paula Whyman.
Description: Evanston, Illinois : TriQuarterly Books/Northwestern University
    Press, 2016.
Identifiers: LCCN 2016001858 | ISBN 9780810133532 (pbk. : alk. paper) |
    ISBN 9780810133549 (e-book)
Classification: LCC PS3623.H94 Y68 2016 | DDC 813.6—dc23
LC record available at http://lccn.loc.gov/2016001858

For my mom and dad,
and
in memory of Bruce

CONTENTS

YOU MAY SEE A STRANGER

DRIVER'S EDUCATION

ACCORDING TO THEIR ads, the Simple Safe Solution Driving School offered classes "at numerous satellite locations in order to serve a larger geographic area." Our classroom was at the end of a deserted corridor in the basement of the Mackleby-Warner department store. At first I thought the basement looked like the set of a slasher movie: the gray tub filled with naked mannequins and spare body parts was the place where the killer hid his victims. Empty plastic hangers stacked to the ceiling on tall, metal poles, and straight pins covering the floor were instruments of torture. If you stepped on the pins just right, they could go through the sole of your shoe. The main level of the store was like the part of the house visitors were allowed to see, everything clean and perfect, with no indication of what might be amiss (ominous music swelling in the background) One. Floor. Below.

On the first night of class, I sat next to Kevin Thorpe by accident, and after that I always sat next to Kevin Thorpe because sitting anywhere else would seem like a slight. And whenever I arrived in class first, he sat down next to me, which made me perspire in the armpits. He was my ideal: blond curly hair, blue eyes, golden tan—California surfer-boy, far from home—and a pimply nose just to make him seem real.

There were other girls in the class. I don't remember them, except that one or two were pretty. There were other boys, too, like the boys who sat in the back of the class, slumped in their seats, laughing at secret jokes, coughing out cuss words when the teacher turned his back. I tried not to look at them when I thought they might see. One of them—I think his name was Todd—was tall and broad, bigger than all the other boys, so he filled the doorway when he walked in. He wore a flannel shirt unbuttoned over a tight, white T-shirt, and he carried a pack of Marlboro Reds in his front pocket. He made Kevin, who had a solid swimmer's build, look like a scarecrow. I wondered if Todd was eighteen or nineteen and hadn't passed the driving test yet. Maybe he went on to take it two or three times, or maybe he never passed. Maybe he's in jail now or on a work-release program; maybe he's straightened himself out, and he'll be at my house next week to patch drywall.

Most of the students were fifteen or sixteen, with learner's permits. I was one of the youngest. We were there because the free driver's ed program available in high school wouldn't fit into our class schedules, which were full of college-prep courses or, I suspect in the case of Todd and a few others, because the high school program had proved insufficient preparation for the test. This class consisted of six weeks of lectures, two nights a week. After you passed a written test, you could move on to the good part—eight on-the-road lessons in a car with dual controls.

The classroom instructor was Mr. White. He was a lean black man, fortyish, who walked with a limp. One leg wouldn't bend all the way at the knee, so when he paced back and forth in front of the class, the strain of lifting the bad leg from the floor and launching it to the

4

next position was visible in the tendons that stood out on his neck. It was September, and the room was hot. A fan oscillated in the corner, but didn't cool anything beyond the chalkboard where Mr. White scribbled complex X-O diagrams, as if a football coach were trying to illustrate the correct way of backing out of a driveway into traffic. Every fifteen seconds or so, the fan would send a small puff of dust from the chalk tray into the air like a smoke signal. It got so I'd wait for it, watch the particles float up then rain down in slow motion, like ash on Pompeii. Each time Mr. White's bad leg came up, we could see where the toe of his boot had dragged through the chalk dust that had been blown to the floor. Finally, he wised up and shifted the position of the chalkboard so the fan couldn't blow on it. Kevin and I snickered behind our hands. This was a bonding moment.

In spite of the heat in the room, Mr. White wore a pinstripe shirt, the sleeves rolled up to mid-forearm, and brown Sansabelt pants. His forehead popped with little beads of sweat, which made him seem intense, although his most frequent facial expression was one of strained tolerance.

Halfway through the second class, he said, "Let's get this outta the way now, so you don't sit there wondering about it instead of absorbing every word I say, 'cause when you're driving, you better hear my voice in your head until your voice has enough experience"—he enunciated each syllable of the word "experience"—"to take over." I can hear his voice in my head right now, but he's not talking about three-point turns.

He sat down on a tall metal stool and, with a grunt, thrust his bad leg out toward us. Then he tapped on his thigh, just above the knee, with a closed fist. It made a sound like hard plastic.

"I got clipped by sniper fire in the village of Quo Luk, Vietnam," he said. "If you think you need to know more than that, ask now. Next topic, lane changes."

There was a hush in the classroom. Someone's stomach growled. What did I know about the Vietnam War? My history class was still talking about the cotton gin. What did I know about getting shot and hobbling around on a plastic leg? I'm still trying to figure it out, my vision admittedly skewed, a cliché fed by years of war movies: Mr. White walks alone on a dusty road, enters a thatched hut village. He sits down on a fallen tree trunk, fumbles for his rations or for a cigarette. His shoes are covered with muck from marching through the jungle. The place is deserted, eerily quiet. The village seems abandoned. Where's the rest of his platoon? He lights his cigarette and notices a shoe in the dirt behind one of the huts, a shoe just like his, but empty, laces cut, in the stained dirt, dirt stained the color of—and right when he realizes he's the only one left, right when he reaches for his gun, a shot comes from nowhere, then another, tearing open his knee. He drops to the ground and hides behind the tree. His mouth twists in angry agony. The blood flows out from between his fingers as he presses his hands to the wound.

My imagination always gets it wrong. He would not have been alone, walking into a village. If he had been alone, he would not have survived.

WEEK TWO WAS eventful. During the break, Kevin asked me out. The class was two hours long, and the break always came halfway through, for twenty minutes. Twenty minutes was a long time. We went upstairs to the shopping level. Kevin bought me green Jelly Bellies, and we played volleyball with a balled up handout about parallel parking at a net that was set up in sporting goods. He told me his parents were divorced, and his mom still lived in California. He wouldn't see her until Thanksgiving. I thought about how all the cool kids I knew—the ones who were allowed to stay out till midnight, who wore designer blue jeans and had brand new

Betamaxes—had divorced parents. But it wasn't their stuff I admired; there was something romantic about their tragic circumstance, the burden borne in solitude, their stoic worldliness. Not that I wanted my parents to divorce, but I tried to picture them living apart, me and my sister going to stay with my dad on weekends. But if one of our parents were always absent, I'd be forced to spend more time alone with my sister, tolerating her moods. And the centrifugal pull of her needs would be doubled, expanding across two households. There was nothing romantic, I realized, about that; I'd only feel more alone. It seemed more appealing to imagine myself as Jane Eyre, with no family at all.

THE STORE CLOSED at 9:00 P.M., but our class wasn't over until 9:30, so each night we exited through the darkened hosiery department, past rows of mannequin legs that had been severed at the knee and sheathed in various opaque shades of pantyhose. In the dark, they stood above the shopping floor like rent-a-cops, oblivious to the low-lifes slipping by in the shadows. I imagined Mr. White's plastic leg standing tall alongside the others, wearing a sheer sandal-toed variety in nude. Gentlemen prefer Hanes.

The first night of week three, the class ran a few minutes late, because Mr. White was going on about the importance of keeping the right amount of empty space in front of you on the highway, one car length for every ten miles of speed. Now, I understand that this will never work, because if you ever have six car lengths ahead of you on I-95, four cars will cut in front of you to fill up the space. But while Mr. White was diagramming car lengths for us, there was a smell of sulfur, and then smoke drifted up from somewhere behind me. I turned around, and it was Todd, sucking on a Marlboro. He narrowed his eyes at me, and I almost looked away. Then, he formed an "O" with his mouth and blew a perfect smoke ring in my direction. Mr. White's voice boomed from the front of the room, and I whipped my head around.

"No smoking during class," he said. This was before the invention of indoor air quality.

"Class is over," said Todd.

"I guess you didn't understand me," said Mr. White. "Put it out, boy."

Everyone watched Todd stand up and shove away an empty desk that blocked the aisle in front of him. The metal feet of the chair screeched against the linoleum at a particularly excruciating pitch. He strutted out the door into the dark corridor. I saw the circle of red on the end of his cigarette recede. When I turned back, Kevin was staring at me. I smiled, but he looked away. A moment later, one of Todd's friends let out a belly laugh. We looked behind us, and in the doorway was a naked mannequin. Todd was hiding in the darkness and with one hand held the mannequin up by its ample and nippleless breast. There was some half-suppressed chuckling and snorting.

"Oh, baby," the mannequin moaned. "You can have the right of way with me." A little puff of cigarette smoke wafted into the room from behind the mannequin's head. There was something else: she was missing a leg.

Mr. White's desk creaked. Like in a tennis match, we all turned to the front to see what he'd do. He swung his leg down from the desk, where he'd been half-sitting. Sweat was popping on his forehead like dew, but being the adult, he exercised self-control.

"Class dismissed," he said quietly, though not the acquiescent or soothing kind of quiet, but rather the kind of quiet that carries a foretaste of menace.

Todd was gone before we reached the hallway. The smell of his smoke still hung in the air.

KEVIN AND HIS dad picked me up in a white '79 Caprice. Kevin sat in front, so I had the whole expanse of back seat to myself. The leather squeaked every time we stopped at a light, and Kevin would turn around and look at me, but we barely talked until we were alone. Ever try to figure out what you talked about on a date when you were fifteen? Rocket science and Great Books, right? While we ate pizza, I asked him about California. He told me about surfing in Malibu and Santa Monica, about the tiny scar on his chin from a bad wipeout, about seeing Victoria Principal walk down the street.

"Is she pretty in person?" I asked.

"Sure," said Kevin. "But I guess she looks better on TV."

Everything does. I always wanted to go to California because I was sure I'd be instantly transformed into a beautiful, golden creature.

We saw *Raiders of the Lost Ark*. I didn't tell Kevin I'd already seen it, but I suspected he had, too. In between the good scenes, he kissed me, perfectly competent, respectful first-date kissing. I thought about Mr. White and his leg. There was no blood in this movie. Did his leg actually get blown off, or was it amputated? Either way, I guessed there would be a lot of blood.

AT THE END of week three, Mr. White showed us slides of drunk driving accidents and talked about the importance of staying sober on the road.

"Drunk driving is no joke," he said. "You drive drunk, best you can do is lose your license. Worst you can do is kill someone, kill yourself."

Todd and his friends coughed behind me: "Bud. J. D. Drink Bud. J. D."

I wondered how Mr. White ended up teaching our class. If he had a teaching certificate, he could have been a "real" teacher; I knew that much back then. Now, I realize he probably was a teacher, moonlighting for the extra cash. Maybe he went to college on the GI Bill when he got home with his medal and his honorable discharge.

Back then, when I imagined what he did in the daytime, I didn't picture him going to work. I figured he slept late, ate corn flakes in his jammies and drew up new diagrams for our class on paper napkins. Or he hung around his apartment in a sleeveless undershirt and boxer shorts, not hiding the plastic leg because there was no one there to see, anyway. Maybe he didn't even put the leg on when he was at home. Maybe he hobbled around on a crutch and sat on the couch watching *Hollywood Squares*, cursing. Why did Paul Lynde always get the center square? Why not Rosey Grier or Nipsey Russell? Why'd they always try to keep the black man down? Or maybe there was somebody there. He didn't wear a ring, but I think he had a lady friend who made him dinner sometimes, and then he didn't take his pants off except in the dark because he hated for her to see the stump. Maybe she waited for him in the dark in a red satin nightie, but after that third week he came home and said, "Not tonight, baby," because he couldn't get Todd's mocking face out of his head. Maybe he got mad and had to go out for a walk so he wouldn't slap her when she went all sympathetic on him. "Tell me about it, honey," she'd say, her eyes puppying up. He hated it when she felt sorry for him because of the leg. And she'd pretend she didn't, insist she didn't, but she really did, really. And she hated when he didn't take it off before they made love, because he was in a hurry or he wanted it for traction. She hated the way the plastic felt rubbing against her thigh, all cold, when the other side was warm, warm, warm.

WEEK FOUR, during a break, Kevin kissed me inside the tent camper that was on display in sporting goods. When we came out, he had his arm around me, and Todd was there, lying on a weight bench and pumping iron, clenching an unlit cigarette between his teeth. A vein bulged in the middle of his forehead, and his face was red with exertion. He'd stripped off the flannel shirt and hung it over the weight stand. I could see the outline of his pectoral muscles and his nipples under the T-shirt. I began to sweat in important places. I wondered if this was how animals felt. I swallowed. Todd's biceps overwhelmed the sleeves of his T-shirt, pushing them back so that when he lifted the weights above his head, I could see the black hair in his armpits. I realized I was an animal. When Todd saw me and Kevin, he curled his lip and snorted. I stood there anyway, staring like an idiot, until Kevin put his hand on my waist and steered me back to the elevator.

"Grit," Kevin muttered. "Grit" was another word for redneck. I wondered if it referred to the breakfast cereal or to the axle grease under their fingernails.

"Do they have grits in California?" I asked.

"No. Just freaks. Potheads. Rednecks only live in the South, not the West."

"This isn't the South," I said. "This is a Mid-Atlantic state."

"Tell the grits that," said Kevin. We were standing near the hanger smokestack. Kevin started to spin the hangers on their pole. "Why do you think Todd hates Mr. White so much?" he said, as if he knew the answer. He had a whole stack spinning at once. It made a loud clatter.

"'Cause White won't let him smoke in the classroom," I said.

"Come on, Miranda," Kevin leaned into me. "It's 'cause he's black."

"No way. He's just bored with the class. It's a boring class."

"You think it's boring?" Kevin looked annoyed.

"The breaks aren't boring," I said.

"I guess not." And he kissed me again. *Come on, baby, surf with me.*

RIGHT TURN ON red. Did I know about that before? I never paid attention when I went places in the car until that class. The meaning of a red light was always unambiguous: you stop. End of story. Now, it seemed, it was okay to go on red, as long as you took some reasonable precautions. Mr. White used the word "judgment."

"You must have good judgment," he said. "Someone could be turning left from across the intersection." He scribbled a diagram on the board. "Or someone could be coming straight across from the left. And who has the right-of-way in that situation? Mr. Thorpe?"

"The driver with the green light always has the right-of-way," said Kevin.

"Anybody wanna disagree with Mr. Thorpe?" Mr. White asked.

A girl in front raised her hand. "But at a four-way stop, the driver on the right has the right-of-way. So maybe the person on the left has to let me go?"

"But you aren't at a four-way stop. You're at a red light. You got no right-of-way at all. The burden's on you to make sure the way is clear. Mr. Thorpe is correct. The driver with the green has the right-of-way. Exceptions, anyone?"

No one raised his hand.

"I'm sure y'all thought this was too obvious to mention," said Mr. White. "A pedestrian in the crosswalk always has the right-of-way. And even when they don't, even if they're jaywalking, you let 'em go. Why?"

Kevin raised his hand again. "Because you don't want to hit a pedestrian."

"'Cause when they're dead, are you gonna feel good that you had the right-of-way? See, I'm not taking anything for granted in this class," said Mr. White. "Let's review. Right turn on red: when to go?"

"When the way is clear," someone said.

"And you use your what? Ms. Weber?"

"Judgment," I said.

"Good judgment is innate," said Mr. White.

"Who's Nate?" asked Todd.

IT WAS OKAY to miss one class without making it up, but you couldn't miss more than one and still graduate to the road lessons. The last night of the fifth week, Kevin missed a class. He had stomach flu. I wondered if I would get it. He'd kissed me the other day in a fitting room during the break. I was about to let him prove that he could undo my bra-hook with one hand, but we got caught by the saleslady in Better Ready-to-Wear. She knocked on the door and asked if I needed any help. Twenty minutes must have seemed like a long time to her, too.

Kevin answered in a falsetto, "No thanks, honey." I smacked him on the arm.

"Everyone's called 'honey' around here," he said afterward.

The night he was sick, he called me at home to say he couldn't come to class, but I'd already left. I wasn't sure what to do at break time without Kevin. A bunch of people were walking to the Orange Bowl for pizza, but I wasn't hungry. I thought about playing basketball in sporting goods, but they'd removed the hoop and replaced it with a dart board. Instead, I haunted the Estée Lauder counter, testing the lavender eye shadow. When I looked in the big round mirror, I could see the reflection of Todd and his friends smoking in the mall, just beyond the store entrance. I sampled some lipstick, "Plum Pretty," and ambled back through sporting goods.

"Hey." I looked around but didn't see anyone. "Babe."

I stopped and put my hands on my hips. "All right. Who's there?"

"It's not Ke-vin," the voice sang. It was coming from the general vicinity of the camping display. I walked slowly in that direction.

"Boo-hoo!" the voice continued. "Loverboy's left you all alone. What will you ever do?"

"Shut up," I said as I got closer.

A cough came from inside the tent camper. "Tough chick. Don't hurt me. Oh, hurt me, please."

I lifted the flap of the tent, and there in the half-light was Todd. "You," I said. "I knew it." I swatted the flap closed and turned to walk away, but Todd was quicker and grabbed my wrist, pulling me into the tent.

He flicked on his cigarette lighter, so I could see his triumphant smile and the dark stubble on his chin. He did not let go of my wrist. "What's the rush? There's ten more minutes." He wasn't wearing a watch, but he was right.

In English class at school, we read *A Streetcar Named Desire*, and there was the part where Stanley says to Blanche, "We've had this date from the beginning." I thought of that when Todd put his other arm around my waist and pulled me against him. I could feel his dick pushing at me from inside his chinos. I giggled. He kissed me short and hard, then backed off. He smelled like cigarettes, but he tasted like Trident. He had chewed gum for me.

"What you laughing at?" he asked. He tossed his head, and his brown forelock swung in front of his eyes.

"I don't think I'm your type, exactly," I said.

"What's my type, exactly, Ms. Weber?"

"You know. Bleached hair, black eyeliner, French-cut jeans. Names like Serena."

"Takes one to know one," he said. He bowed his head to suck on my collarbone where it was revealed at the open neck of my polo shirt and worked his way up to whisper in my ear. "So, that's why we're here," he said, as his hand slithered under my shirt, "'cause I like slutty chicks, not prissy-ass goody-goods." He licked my ear.

"And you like Kevins." He straightened up suddenly and stared down at me. "I'm a dumb redneck to you, right, babe?" Without warning, he reached out with the hand that wasn't around my breast and brushed my hair out of my face, tucking it behind my ear in a way that was at once overly familiar and oddly tender. Now, when men do that to me I want to shrug them away. But when he did it, I couldn't say anything. I was having a rare epiphany. Todd, I realized, was a fraud. And it really was easy to unhook my bra one-handed.

Then he kissed me again, and if Kevin kissed like a fish, a teasing nibble here and there, Todd was a shark, carnivorous, devouring. I would sit in class for the rest of the evening feeling like I was covered with a protective film of Todd, and at the same time feeling like I had him inside me, because when I breathed, it was his breath that came out of my mouth, and when I swallowed, it was his spit that ran down the back of my throat.

When I stepped out of the tent to go to class, I saw Mr. White limping by on his way to the elevator. He nodded to me as he passed. Todd came out behind me, and I thought I saw Mr. White's eyes get narrow. Todd had a Plum Pretty face. Ten minutes could be a long time.

Todd missed the next class. I heard he had stomach flu.

THE LAST NIGHT of class, everyone was there. I sat with Kevin like always, but I could feel Todd eyeballing me from behind. What if he said something? I didn't want to hurt Kevin's feelings, and anyway fooling around with Todd didn't mean anything, not really.

Mr. White told us he'd review everything during the first half of class, and after the break, we would take the written test. If we passed, we could go on to the road lessons. He was going over the part about emergency handling and accident avoidance.

"That's right. Always turn the wheel in the direction of the skid," he said. "And how do you avoid the most common type of accident?"

"Keep enough space between you and the car in front of you," said Kevin.

"Dork," coughed the boys in back.

"Right on, Mr. Thorpe," said Mr. White. "And what do you do if someone cuts you off?"

"Slow down to maintain your distance," someone said.

"Flip him the bird," said Todd. "Ram his ass."

"Beat his brains out," said one of Todd's friends.

"Blow his legs off," said another.

"Slow down," Mr. White wrote on the board in large letters and circled it. Then he turned quickly, grimacing with the effort of propelling his leg around, and stood glaring at the back of the class. After a moment of silence in which we all had a chance to read the doom imprinted on his brow, he said, "Get. Out." He didn't shout or lose control. "You. You. You," he pointed. "Outta here. Now."

Todd's friends looked like they hadn't heard right. "What about the test?" asked Todd.

"Now you're worried about the test?" Mr. White shook his head in frustration. "Take it from somebody else. Make an appointment at the central office. I don't care. Get out of my classroom."

We stared at the three of them while they stood up and shoved their chairs over, lit their cigarettes, and headed for the door. They took their time leaving so they could smoke and flick their ashes on the floor. One of them muttered, "Fuckin' nigger," on his way out, loud enough for everyone to hear. The collective gasp of the class in response seemed to suck all the air out of the room. I was sure it wasn't Todd. When they were finally gone, and we could all exhale, Kevin reached over and squeezed my leg to say "I told you so."

Mr. White sat down heavily on the desk, resting his bad leg on a chair, and stared into the space between him and all of us. I felt sorry for him, more sorry than I felt about his leg. He didn't say anything. No one did. A few minutes later, he called the break. It was early, but he said we'd had enough reviewing; we were ready for the test.

Kevin and I stood in the corridor with the rest of the class, waiting for the elevator. "Do you wanna study during the break?" he asked.

"I don't think we need to, do you?"

"No," said Kevin. "Wanna go camping?" That was his cute way of saying he wanted to fool around. He put his hand on the back of my neck and left it there. It made me feel a little like a dog on a choke chain. I didn't know what to say. I was half-afraid we'd open the tent flap and find Todd in there. Was Todd right about me? Was I a Todd-kind-of-girl or a Kevin-kind-of-girl? Why did I feel like I had to choose? Did anyone else have to? While I was figuring it out, the doors opened, and there was Todd standing in the elevator instead, smacking his palm with a brand new baseball bat from sporting goods. He looked at me and then at Kevin. I didn't meet his eyes but watched the muscles move smoothly under the skin of his forearm as he raised and lowered the bat.

"Shit," said Kevin, not moving except to lift his hand off my neck.

"What the hell?" It was Mr. White's voice coming from somewhere behind me, and before I had a chance to tell Kevin that the tent sounded pretty good about now, Mr. White growled, "Outta my way," and we all got out of his way. Kevin took me by the arm and dragged me backwards so fast I almost fell on the floor. We stood with our backs pressed against the mannequin dumpster.

"You want a piece of me, you dumbass? You want a piece of me?" Mr. White had instantly assumed this martial-arts-type stance, his fists gathered up near his collar in a pre-strike position. He stood with his legs apart, not at all clumsy on the fake one. "You think you can take me?" Mr. White hissed. "I'm trained in hand-to-hand combat, you white fucking trailer trash."

Todd's eyes widened, as if he'd temporarily blacked out and come to holding the bat with no idea how he got there. I had a sudden image of his parents at home. There was his dad, the biceps all gone to fat around a tattoo of a fiery cross, nailing AstroTurf to the front stoop with a staple gun, while his mom chucked the broken toaster out on the lawn next to the broken TV set.

"Holy shit," Kevin whispered excitedly. "This is gonna be like Bruce Lee."

"They've had this date from the beginning," I said.

"What?" said Kevin.

Sometimes in movies, the fight scenes happen in slow motion, and that's how it seemed to me when I watched Todd and Mr. White. Even though it was over in a matter of seconds, the whole scene plays back slow and dreamy in my mind's eye.

Todd stepped off the elevator and paused as if he hadn't planned on this course of action at all but felt compelled toward it now like a salmon who suddenly realizes how stupid it is to swim upstream yet can't quite stop itself all the same, and then he swung the bat at Mr. White's head. I'm guessing that Todd had a good five inches and forty pounds on Mr. White. He missed anyway. The two men circled, with Todd taking another swing and Mr. White ducking to avoid the bat, his fake knee bending ever so slightly. Then, Mr. White made his move. It was so fast that even though I was watching the whole time, I felt like I didn't see it happen. When Todd swung the bat again, Mr. White grabbed it with both hands. Todd hung on, and Mr. White whomped him in the chest with the handle of the bat, knocking the wind out of him. Now, I'm thinking that the only reason Mr. White didn't bat him in the nose when he had the chance was that he was trying not to draw blood. Anyway,

Todd was on the ground hyperventilating. Mr. White stood over him until he looked like he was going to catch his breath, and then Mr. White was on him, pinning him to the linoleum by pressing the side of the bat against his neck and his good knee in Todd's crotch. I tried not to remember the feeling of that crotch grinding against me on the floor of the tent. Todd grabbed for Mr. White's neck, squeezing the veins that stood out there as Mr. White pressed down on the bat. He held on briefly, his arms shuddering with the effort, but finally he had to let go. Todd was struggling to breathe, his eyes bulging out, when Mr. White leaned in real close to his face and cleared his throat, as if he was about to hock a big loogie on Todd's cheek. But he didn't.

"You'll be glad to see the cops, won't you?" Mr. White said. "Someone call the police," he ordered.

"Come on," said Kevin, grabbing me by the wrist.

"Wait a minute," I said.

"Come on," he repeated, dragging me past the rest of the students who were standing around gawking, and past Todd, who was making gurgling sounds from underneath the bat. I hated to see him like that. His eyes, wet and startled, flitted to me as I walked by, but I pretended not to notice.

"Can you believe how White took him down? Man, that was awesome," said Kevin.

Upstairs, we walked to the make-up counter, and Kevin asked the saleslady to call the police. I put on some misty-blue eye shadow.

"Do you think we still have to take the test?" I asked.

"Maybe they'll pass us all because of emotional trauma," said Kevin.

It ended up we had to take the test by appointment at the Simple Safe Solution offices. I half-expected to see Todd there. I still didn't think he had called Mr. White the Name. I wonder if he ever showed up.

After the class was over, Kevin called me a couple of times and asked me out, but I made up excuses.

ABOUT A MONTH AGO, I stopped into Mackleby-Warner. I hadn't been there in years, since I got married and moved from the neighborhood and divorced. I was driving back from the lawyer's office, George Thorogood howling on the oldies station, when I passed the store and pulled an illegal U-turn into the lot. I saw right away that the whole place had gone downhill. All the fabrics looked too shiny and cheap, the lighting was too bright and yellow, and the carpet was gray and unraveling. On a whim, I went to the cosmetics counter and put on the thickest, blackest eyeliner I could find. I prowled the sporting goods department, not really looking for the tent camper, I told myself, and the place where I thought it had been was stacked with paintball guns and inline skates. There was a hoop, though, so I shot a few baskets.

I walked out onto the mall past some guys who were hunched over their cigarettes, slouching against the wall. Not much had changed, after all. As I passed, I heard a tar-laden voice say, "Babe," and I half-turned, not even half, just enough to see if he meant me.

DROSOPHILA

MR. PIERSON, MY twelfth-grade biology teacher, is unmarried and has blond hair growing on his knuckles. We used to say hair on the knuckles was a sign of mental retardation, but my mother made me stop saying that a long time ago, because of my sister. Donna has no hair on her knuckles, but that never stopped the other kids from telling me my sister's a retard. My mother said to tell them it takes one to know one.

My sister is not a retard; she's a fruit fly, *Drosophila melanogaster*. I watch the wingless one that's shuffling around on the food supply inside the Mason jar, its toes dipped in a loam of rotting pear, lemon rind, souped banana. If I'm to be my sister's keeper, best to keep her in a Mason jar. I can watch her if I want, and I can put her on a shelf and go away whenever I like.

WHEN I WAS younger and my friends came to visit, my mother would say, "Include your sister," but Donna didn't wait for an invitation. She followed me from room to room, a ghost in white tennis socks with pink puff balls at the heels and a nightgown she wore all day if she didn't go out. On the front of the gown was a picture of the yellow-haired specter of Cinderella, peeling off in flakes like lead paint. Now that Donna's twenty-two, it's hard to find a Cinderella nightgown that fits her, so our mother sends away in the mail for a decal and irons it on herself. Donna has a burn on her thigh from years ago when she tugged on the iron's cord. I was too young to remember.

HEAT-TRAPPED PHEROMONES mean the smell in the jar is equal parts fruit and spunk, with a hint of vanilla, or maybe that's a scent reference to the memory of my mother's rice pudding from last night's dinner, blanaxed by the lingering taste of my boyfriend, Victor. I just spent a half hour of my free period with Victor, inside the shed where they keep outdoor gym equipment—tackle dummies and lacrosse sticks, sod and leather and damp athlete-armpit. It was unseasonably cold, and I'd forgotten my gloves, so he warmed my hands under his sweatshirt first. I've never actually put his dick in my mouth, but I was curious and licked my fingers after he came. He didn't see me do it.

To prepare the female for copulation, the male *D. melanogaster* licks the female's genitalia. I think about suggesting this to Victor, but right now, I'm only that bold in my mind. We're both virgins, and we're not in a hurry to change that.

D. MELANOGASTER IS the perfect creature for genetic analysis. It turns out that we're half fruit fly—the nonflying half, the half that thinks about food and sex and sex and food. In my jar, eggs are constantly hatching. Each female lays up to one hundred eggs in a day, and the eggs hatch in twelve hours. The larvae eat and molt, eat and molt, and then they pupate for a few days before emerging as adults. One of my assignments is to produce grids called

Punnett squares that predict the genetic make-up of offspring of selected flies in my jar.

The genes of the fruit fly were named whimsically, according to their functions, as if the scientists felt like playing a practical joke. There is, for instance, a gene that will result in a fruit fly that's born without a heart. It's called Tin Man. There are three genes whose proportionate presence determine a fly's sex: One is called Sisterless; another is Sex-Lethal; the third is Deadpan. They sound like the names of punk bands: Deadpan, opening for the Sex Pistols. Sisterless, double-bill with Black Flag. I draw Punnett squares demonstrating how these three genes interact. As a female fruit fly, I would be Sisterless. And so would my sister, in case it's not already confusing enough. When the Sex-Lethal gene is minimized, the fruit flies are male.

I should warn Victor that I'm Sex-Lethal, but when we're together my mouth is busy with his, his early mustache abrades the skin above my lip, and my hands are caught up in his soft curly hair. Everything about him is going from soft to hard, not only his dick, but his arms, his thighs. Not his eyes, though. His eyes stay soft when he looks at me.

There are more fruit flies each time I check. It's becoming difficult to keep track of the numbers, to note how many have white eyes, how many brown, vermillion, yellow, how many are males, how many are blind—only one so far. I count the dead ones, too. Some of the larvae die before pupating. Over time, the food supply becomes littered with their small dark bodies, like poppy seeds. Some of the adults also die in the food, but most are stiff in the bottom of the jar, their legs folded inward over their bellies.

Do the hatchlings see my giant head hovering above from inside their shells before they emerge? Do I appear to them like a storm cloud or the onset of night?

DONNA SHUFFLES, walking on the balls of her feet, as if she's perpetually about to go up on tiptoe. The doctor says her Achilles tendons are tight from a kind of palsy. They don't know what kind. They don't know anything about why my sister is the way she is—slow but not entirely stupid, with fingers that don't work as well as they should. She wears shoes that slip on or buckle because she can't keep them tied.

"Fine motor skills," my mother says.

The physical therapist wanted Donna to practice working her hands and building the muscles in her arms and wrists. Donna was already fourteen when she was given a Stretch Armstrong doll, the one that looks like a squat bodybuilder. The doll is filled with a thick gel that gives, with effort, when you squeeze it or poke it hard. Its name comes from the fact that you can pull the arms and legs out absurdly far, and when you stop, they slowly return to their original shape and size. Donna loved Stretch Armstrong the way some girls love their Barbies. Every morning, she made her bed, pulled up the bedspread crooked but neat, and sat Stretch on her pillow alone, like a king. Every night, she propped him on a chair in sight of her bed, before she went to sleep.

DONNA DOESN'T HAVE the square head and thick tongue; some of her friends do. They're like big puppies—when I see them they're always happy. Their nasal, phlegmy voices scare me. They talk like someone is clinging to their tongues. My sister doesn't sound like that, but she speaks in a monotone, even when she's excited. She used to get excited when the mailman delivered sample boxes of new breakfast cereals with the mail. The mailman taught me how to roller skate. He tried to teach Donna, but gave up. She puts on the skates anyway and clomps around on the grass.

Back then, when I was ten or so, my friend Karen would come

over and we'd entertain ourselves thinking of ways to torture my sister. No other fifth-grader I knew could make her teenage sister cry. Sometimes I could do it just by hiding my face and then suddenly looking up and shouting at her. The first time, Karen stared like I'd drowned a kitten. I felt bad that Donna was crying. I tried to distract her by making a face, pushing up the tip of my nose so my nostrils flared like a pig nose, and rolling my eyes back to expose the whites. Donna went instantly from crying to laughing. Karen let me have some of her Girl Scout cookies.

"Maybe I should give one to Donna," Karen said.

"No, don't," I whispered. "She's not allowed to eat cookies."

I'M GOING TO college next year. Victor's going, too, but he's going far away, and I'm only going across town. I picture the scene as if he's walking off down an endless, empty road. The tail of his rugby shirt rides up above his butt, like always. I put my hand in the back pocket of his jeans, and he puts his hand in my back pocket, and we lean on each other as we walk, stopping to kiss in front of the neighbor's house when we know she's watching out the window. But this time will be different. We'll never see each other again. I say that to him, now and then, with a downcast face, a sad look in my eye. It feels like I'm practicing being romantic. I don't know why I can't feel it for real; it's like I'm only watching. The same way I watch the fruit flies. Which one of them is me? And immediately, I know: It's the black-eyed one that never lands anywhere for long.

Someday, when I consider having children, I decide I'll make Punnett squares plotting the possible offspring of me and my husband, taking my sister's genes into account, the ones that could be hiding, unexpressed, behind my own. I'll concern myself with the uncertainty that resides between the lines on the grid. Is there a gene for wearing your nightgown all day? A gene that makes you drink the bottle of Woolite your mother keeps under the bathroom sink? I heard my mother whisper to my father on the phone, "Did she think she was drinking bleach?"

What is recessive? Fear is dominant. But for now I'm thinking about being stuck inside a jar.

When I tell Victor these are our last few months together, he says I'm being melodramatic, but I know I'm right. This is one of my strengths, being right even when it's not in my favor. Because despite feeling separate, I don't want to give him up. Maybe separate is a good way to be. Otherwise when he goes away, he'll take me with him, and then what will be left of me?

My other strength is kissing. Victor says I'm a good kisser. I tell him I was taught by a redneck. I don't tell him that. I say, "It's because I'm kissing you." He pretends to believe me.

I put a dark cloth over the jar of fruit flies so they'll settle down, like birds. When I uncover it, I have a couple of minutes to count them before they start flying around again.

DONNA'S SOCIAL CLUB meets every Friday. Sometimes they go bowling; sometimes they go to the movies. The goal is to have them do things that normal people would do, but with each other, to help them make friends, yes, and also because normal people won't do those things with them unless they get paid. There was a woman who used to come to our house to try and teach Donna to cook. When my mother was out, this woman took four fresh steaks from our fridge and hid them in the clothes dryer. She meant to take them home with her but she forgot. We found them by the smell. A man who was supposed to drive Donna home from her social club outings stole money from Donna's wallet. Now I drive her. I take Victor along because it gives us more time together, and he doesn't mind.

He's nice. I'm nice, too, mostly. We don't smoke or drink or get high like a lot of the other seniors.

This Friday, Donna's club is having a dance. The hall where the dance takes place is decorated with balloon arches, silver streamers curling down from the ceiling, and gold confetti settled like dandruff on the tables. When we arrive, Joe Cocker is singing about being lifted up where he belongs. Outside the social hall, Victor and I hold each other and sway until the end. I like my face in his neck, where I can feel his pulse and inhale what I think his pillow smells like. *Life's you and I / Alive, today.* I put my hand under his shirt in back and run my fingers along the knobs of his spine, until he stops me because it tickles.

There's a buffet table. I pick grapes off of a stem, and Victor spears tiny orange cheddar squares with toothpicks. We eat Ritz crackers that make our lips feel buttery, and we talk with our mouths full. I drop a few grapes into my purse for *D. melanogaster.*

"You're like my grandmother," says Victor. He wraps some cheese in a napkin and hands it to me.

"That's okay," I say. "Cheese will go sour."

There must be thirty people on the dance floor, the most I've ever seen at one of these events. I search for my sister among them. Because they're handicapped, I think of these people as children, though all are several years older than me. The men and their lumbering pace, their lack of rhythm, isn't that different from the way normal boys dance. There's a Down syndrome man in the center of the dance floor, wearing a cowboy hat, the pearly snaps on his shirt undone, his undershirt plastered with sweat. He twirls his partner and lifts her off the ground. Other dancers back away to give them space. The crowd makes a circle around them and everyone applauds.

"At least Donna has someplace to go," says Victor, "with people." He means "people like her."

But I think Donna would rather be around normal people. Sometimes she locks herself in her room and refuses to go to her social club outings, or anywhere at all. I wish I knew how much she understands about herself.

I finally spot her on the far edge of the dance floor. She's drinking Pepsi from a can through a straw and rocking back and forth in an approximation of the rhythm. She's alone. She wears a fuzzy peach sweater and a long black skirt. I recognize the sweater but decide not to mention it. I want Victor to keep thinking I'm a good person. I circumnavigate the dance floor. Victor follows me.

"You look pretty," I say.

"It's not time to leave yet," says Donna. There's an absence in Donna's face. The way I think of it, she's missing from herself. Is there a gene for "all there"? Is there an official diagnosis, Not-All-There Syndrome?

"We'll wait," I say. "Are you going to do some dancing? I know you like this song." They're playing "Karma Chameleon."

"The dance is over in fifteen minutes," she says. "We can leave in fifteen minutes." The rules are important to her.

"Are your friends here?" I say. Victor, who has been holding my hand, tugs on it lightly and tries to catch my eye. I disengage my hand.

"There are no cute boys," she says.

"Who are you hanging out with," I say.

"Can I have more tiny cakes?" she says.

On a nearby table there's a large tray of petit fours. Some of the cakes are missing their iced tops, as if they've been picked off. "It's up to you," I say.

Victor holds his hand out to me. "Care to dance?"

I look at the damaged people shimmying around the dance floor. I don't feel right leaving Donna alone at her own dance. "No, thanks." But I take Victor's hand anyway and kiss his fingers.

Donna giggles. "You guys!" she says. "Someone'll see you."

I used to wonder if Donna had ever had sex. I asked her once, and she said, "Miranda! I'm not married!"

I wish I had a sister I could talk to.

I lean over and whisper in Victor's ear, "Ask Donna to dance."

Victor's a nice person, like I said, and still he looks like he'd rather I asked him to dance with my mother.

I nudge him. I stuff cheese cubes into my cheeks until they puff out, and I make gerbil noises. Donna points and snort-laughs at me. Victor nods. He's going to do it.

The theme from *Flashdance* is playing. As soon as the slow verse gives way to the buoyant chorus, there's wild jumping and arm-flapping. Victor turns to Donna and holds his elbow out. "Let's dance," he says.

She takes a long slurp through her straw, then hands me the can of Pepsi. "Don't let them throw it away," she says.

She hops ahead of Victor to the center of the dance floor, below the revolving light ball. Victor isn't a bad dancer, and he's making an effort. He only turns away once to wink at me. Donna shuffles from side to side, flailing her arms like she's scattering rice after a wedding. On the chorus—*Being's believing / I can have it all!*—Victor grabs one of her hands and spins her, like a faltering top. Her mouth hangs open, and I can tell she's concentrating on keeping herself upright.

In one of the more awkward segues in deejay history, the end of *Flashdance* bleeds into the beginning of "Every Breath You Take." Victor stops, waiting for Donna to stop and, I guess, wondering whether he's fulfilled his duty. My sister continues bobbing and shuffling and wagging her head back and forth, only a little more slowly to acknowledge the change in tempo. Victor glances at me, and I give him the head signal that means he can come back now. But he doesn't leave the dance floor. He takes Donna's hand in his and puts

29

it on his shoulder. He holds her other hand out to the side and puts his free hand on her waist. She stops bobbing and looks down at her feet. Keeping her at arm's length, Victor steps right and back and left, pulling her along with him. Donna raises Victor's hand along with her own and pumps the air, incongruous to the music, as if they're signaling a truck driver to sound his horn.

Then I see my sister look at the couples around them who are draped over each other, rocking slowly in each other's arms. She removes her hand from Victor's shoulder and puts it around his waist instead and hugs him to her, her cheek mashing into his collarbone. I can see his face, a big red question mark hovering above her head. *I'll be watching you . . .* He gives her a quick peck on the crown.

When the song ends, they walk back to me. Donna takes her soda can from my hand.

"Say thank you to Victor," I tell her, and she does.

Victor says, "Thank *you*, Donna. The man should say thank you for a dance." He looks pointedly at me. What have I done wrong now?

Donna presses on my shoulder and loud-whispers into my ear, "Your boyfriend likes me, Miranda." As if he isn't standing right there. Victor grins despite himself.

I nod and say, "Of course he does."

Donna frowns and takes my hand in hers. She pats it in a way that she means to be consoling, but it feels more like she's trying to kill a mosquito. "Don't worry, Miranda," she says. "You'll get another boyfriend. You always do."

"Right-o," says Victor. He turns away from us and walks toward the exit, stopping at the buffet to sweep up a handful of cheese, not bothering with the toothpicks. I watch his shirttail ride up above his butt.

"Oh, come on," I call after Victor. He knows Donna doesn't understand what she's saying. Doesn't he?

What will happen when Victor goes away? I mistakenly believe that he's my conscience, and when he leaves, there's no telling what I might do.

I grab Donna's face, my hands on her cheeks squeezing a little too hard at first. I bring her face to mine, and I kiss her in the center of her forehead, where our mother says the invisible evil eye resides. It keeps me from saying the things that want to come out of my mouth.

"You're embarrassing me," Donna says, and pulls away.

AFTER I SHOWED Karen how I could make Donna laugh and cry on command, I told her I could make Stretch Armstrong bleed real blood. While Donna was having her fingers manipulated by a physical therapist in the family room, I borrowed Stretch from her bedroom. Karen and I took turns poking him with different objects to see what would create a puncture wound. We settled on the pushpins I used to tack up my autographed photo of the Bay City Rollers. We stabbed Stretch in the lungs and the belly and the biceps, and squeezed until yellow goo came out. We dared each other to taste it, but neither of us would. I pierced the smooth skin between his legs and pressed on his abdomen.

"Look, he's peeing," said Karen.

When we returned Stretch to his place of honor, he was gaunt, his face elongated and thin, a doll Modigliani. We waited in my room for Donna to come upstairs and find him. When we heard her scream and run back down the stairs, I nearly peed myself laughing. After a few days, Donna forgot why I was being punished. My worst punishment is that I can never forget it.

Donna was given a new Stretch Armstrong. The old one stayed hidden in her closet until years later, when my parents cleaned out her things.

"Let the colony expire," Mr. Pierson tells me.

The smell in the jar has developed a sour edge, like grapefruit, and there are too many males, and fewer and fewer females, though the ones that are left are still laying eggs. I don't want to kill them. The wingless female has outlived the rest of her brood by two days so far. I don't think I'll ever understand what's adaptive about winglessness.

A day later, I find blue mold growing in the loam, and the smell has turned to turpentine. The wingless fruit fly is dead, stuck in the brown gruel that used to be a banana.

I decide that on Friday, I'll terminate the colony. Mine is now the only jar left on the windowsill, not because I applied any special techniques in raising my fruit flies, but because I kept sneaking them fresh food after I was supposed to stop. The two grapes I'd saved from Donna's dance had been their last meal.

When I arrive in the classroom on Friday morning, the jar is gone. Mr. Pierson sits at his desk grading papers, and he doesn't look when I walk over to the window. I know he did it, but what's the point of saying anything? I stand in the same place I would have to watch *D. melanogaster*. I stare out the window at the empty bus lane in front of the school, and I think that soon enough I'll be gone from here, too. I can see myself in the glass, and with the driveway beyond, my face appears to float on the asphalt. I'm reminded of the sidelight by the front door of our house. When we were little kids, Donna and I would make a game of looking through the Flemish glass and guessing whose silhouette we saw waiting outside the door. The mailman was brown with a hunchback that was really his mailbag; our father was a black blur with a black hat; our babysitter was tall and curvy and blue and blonde. What did I look like waiting outside the door? I'd never thought to ask my sister.

YOU MAY SEE A STRANGER

POGO WANTS TO pay for everyone. It's a big night for him, and he's taking us to the country club. Cheever and his girlfriend are coming, too. Cheever is Pogo's younger brother. Their father's name is on a plaque somewhere in the building.

"On a bar stool," Pogo joked.

"His name is the same as yours," Cheever told him.

Pogo has wads of cash in his pocket. I have a small square of paper in my purse. It's proof of something that I don't quite believe. When the doctor said it, I thought of an incubator and chicks, my body as a holding area, warm, but like everything else, temporary. Pogo will eventually show everyone the cash. I don't plan to show anyone the paper. This is Pogo's big night, not mine. One big night at a time seems like a good philosophy.

Cheever and Natasha are already at the bar when we arrive. Natasha's glass is full and sweating in her hand. She swirls the yellow straw between her fingers. Cheever orders a gin and tonic for himself. He and Pogo don't look like brothers, but they look related.

They slap each other on the back with friendly hostility, which leads into a wrestler-grip hug held a few beats too long.

"I'm proud of you," says Cheever. He tries to mess Pogo's hair, but Pogo blocks him. Pogo tries to mess Cheever's hair instead, except he can't because it's short and bristly, so it ends up looking like a plush carpet you stroked in the wrong direction.

Pogo orders drinks for both of us. He's had two already, before we got here. One before we got in the car, and one he finished on the way to the club, while I drove. His cheeks and his nose are pleasantly red.

At the bar, I hold up the car key for him to take, and he shows me his pocket. I reach over to slip the key into his khakis, and he grabs my fingers.

"The other one," he whispers in my ear.

I put the key in his other pocket, on the side facing away from Cheever and Natasha, the side without the wad of cash in it. I reach all the way in to stroke him through the lining of his pocket. He isn't wearing underwear. I can feel the hard curve of him. If I try, I think I can feel his blood rushing. He keeps talking, leaning up against the bar. He leans toward Natasha. While he talks, he touches her with his hand that holds the drink, as if he might rest the glass on her shoulder. I squeeze a little. He flinches in a way only I would notice, and he has to stop my hand and shift himself. All this he does seamlessly, while holding the drink in the other hand and expounding on the vagaries of the market.

POGO HAS AN old Mercedes. His father has one, too. His affection for old things confuses me—some are quality, and some are just old. The idea is to look like they don't care about money, or even think about it. If you've had enough of it for a long enough time, say, generations, you don't think about it in the same way as other people.

But that's someone else's money, and whenever Pogo manages to get his own, he wants everyone to know. In my family, what modest funds my parents earned were spent on my sister's doctors and life-skills counselors, and on the annual summer jaunt to a nearby mountain lodge, where Donna and I counted dead flies on the windowsill and held our noses against the smell of the septic tank. We'd never had the luxury to act like we didn't worry.

ON THE WAY to the club, Pogo and I stopped in the parking lot of Broder's, the gourmet grocery store. We shut off the car engine, but left the radio on. We parked at the far end of the lot, but I could still see people coming and going, pushing their carts, which were smaller and daintier than the carts at a run-of-the-mill store.

I didn't want to mess up my skirt by hiking it up to my waist, so I took it off. Pogo tilted the passenger seat back as far as it would go, and I straddled him. It was cramped, and I had to hunch my shoulders to avoid hitting the ceiling. At one point, I leaned forward all the way and lay on top of him, and he pushed me up with his pelvis and shouted "giddyap." He can be a goof that way. I was so high up, I thought later about my naked bottom and the car's moon roof, and shouldn't I laugh about it? But I wasn't exactly thinking about it at the time. A vibration was beginning inside of me, like the background hum of an amplifier. Clapton was singing, *Nobody's lucky till luck comes along / Nobody's lonely till somebody's gone.* That's when I came. Pogo already had, a moment before. It was still daylight.

I wasn't into it at first, doing it outside of Broder's, or even at all. Pogo could nearly always persuade me; he knew and I knew that I would end up feeling like it before he was done. After that, I drove us to the club. The thrumming in my body continued to reverberate, in seeming rhythm with the rattling diesel engine. I wanted to be still for a while longer and let it finish whatever it was doing to me.

Pogo said, "'You, in the cheaper seats, clap your hands; the rest of you just rattle your jewelry.'" This was John Lennon at the Beatles' royal command performance, Pogo was fond of reminding me.

"Am I the queen?" I asked.

"You are the queen of all you survey," said Pogo. In his way, he meant it.

"The Broder's parking lot?" I said.

"Your fiefdom."

"Are you my serf?" I asked.

"I serf no one," said Pogo.

"Ugh," I said.

When we got to the club, I went to the ladies' room. There were hand towels made of the same fabric you'd make cloth napkins out of, folded in rows on a table near the sink. I wanted to bring one into the stall with me to clean up from preceding events. I couldn't though, because there was a black woman sitting on a chair in the room, wearing what looked like a nurse's uniform. She was an attendant. I wasn't sure what she was going to do for me, and I didn't have time to figure it out. My insides felt shaken up and rearranged, and standing in that dim room with the slightly antiseptic odor tipped the balance toward one arrangement rather than another. I bent over the toilet, my bare knees pressed into the knobby floor, and waited. I threw up, and then threw up again. After a while, it stopped on its own, and I sat on the rim in a weakened state, leaning to one side so that I could feel the cool wall tiles. I could fool myself that I was empty, if only for a moment. I had a vision of my body turned inside out, gleaming pink, pristine. So much for that. My knees hurt, as if I'd knelt in pebbles. I sat for as long as I thought I could, awaiting with dread the attendant's tap on the stall door or Pogo's voice outside the ladies' room calling to me. At that moment, nothing seemed more difficult than leaving the bathroom.

Finally, I emerged from the stall. The attendant handed me a cup with green liquid in it. I looked at her questioningly, but she kept her face neutral and turned away. I smelled it; it was mouthwash. She probably thought I was drunk, like the other girls that men try to impress, bringing them to the club for drinks before they get them into bed. But Pogo had done things in reverse, as usual. He didn't have to get me drunk first. He didn't even have to impress me.

After I washed my hands, the woman handed me a towel. There was no place for tips, so I figured that wasn't done. There was a large wicker basket where I finally realized I was supposed to put the used cloth after I dried my hands. I smiled at her and said, "Thank you" when I left the bathroom.

She must be keeping things clean between customers. For some reason, I imagine that she's never permitted to leave the building; perhaps she can't even leave the ladies' room. I wonder if anyone on the outside knows about this, or if it's a secret the members are expected to keep. She's the only black person I'll see at the club tonight.

AT THE CLUB'S BAR, I don't touch my drink right away. I'm not sure how much I want to drink. Same way I was unsure about having sex earlier. I'm resolutely not focusing on the possible reason. Pogo puts the glass in my hand: "Drink the potion," he says. He's always paying attention to how much other people drink. I know I'll oblige. I wonder if Pogo would still give me a drink if he knew. I can't imagine him suddenly becoming responsible. This is, after all, what I both want and don't want about him.

Pogo's ten years older than me. Most men his age are married. He thinks that I won't push him. I play along. I'm only a year out of school, but it's as if I'm the grown-up. Pogo wants to be a kid forever.

My doctor asked me, is the father someone you're serious with? I said yes. Then he'll do right by you, the doctor said. I laughed. The doctor looked at me sadly then. If that were the case, I wouldn't be pregnant. Or I suppose when I forgot to take my pill, I could have said no. When Pogo said, just this one time, please? We'd been dating a year, and up to that time I'd been very good about remembering it. I thought one time would be okay. And maybe it would have been. But if I'm honest I'll also admit it was not just one time.

If we had a boy, first Pogo would teach him how to pee on the side of the road. Then he would teach him persuasion. These are not bad things to know, just as it's not bad sometimes to let yourself be persuaded.

I stare at the coaster my drink has been sitting on. It's the most substantial paper coaster I've ever seen, as thick as a whole pad of paper. Someone spent a lot of money on those. Worth it? I imagine the talk: "Our golf course is first rate, but you should see our coasters—a well-kept secret." Along with the black woman in the bathroom. The club's fleur-de-lis symbol is embossed in gold in the center of the coaster. There's a wet ring where my drink was. But the water doesn't get absorbed, it sits on top. The fleur-de-lis reminds me of something. Sex-flower. Flower of lascivious pomposity. I make these phrases in my head; I entertain myself that way. The same symbol is on the hand towels in the bathroom. I almost cleaned myself with the seal of the King of France.

It's easier to talk to Cheever and Natasha when they've had a couple of drinks, as if they discover their personalities. Maybe they think I'm the same. They're talking about Pogo's big news, except he doesn't want to tell the whole story yet. He's waiting for the moment of utmost drama, so he only drops teasers like, "Do you know how much cash I have in my pocket right now?"

I make a face that tells Cheever and Natasha that I know the answer, and won't they be impressed? Pogo winks at me, commiserating. We're like Penn and Teller.

"I hope it's more than you have in your bank account," says Cheever.

POGO SHOWED ME the money when we were in the car. He used the same line with me: "Do you know how much cash I have in my pocket right now?" This was right before we had sex.

The money was rolled into a thick wad held tight by a rubber band. "I thought you were just happy to see me," I said. "How much is that?"

"Six thousand right here," he said, squeezing it in his fist. "The rest is being held at the firm. Earnest money. The importance of being earnest."

"Are you supposed to have all that?"

"It's mine, all mine," he laughed maniacally and sipped his drink, which was in a real glass he'd brought from home. He's the only person I've ever seen do that, bring a drink in an open glass in a car that isn't a limo. But I never saw Pogo or any of his friends without a drink, a wisecrack, or a woman. They were not-quite Southerners in the not-quite South, pretend gentility and bad behavior coexisting without any apparent discomfort, like Pogo's dress-code-correct pressed khakis with no boxers underneath.

"This is chump change," he said. "After the sale, I get more. A lot more." He unfurled the wad and started peeling off bills. There were fifties and hundreds. His pants were on, but my skirt was already off. I was stretched out next to him, reclining as best I could in the driver's seat, the steering wheel preventing much range of motion. He laid one bill after another side to side, flat on my thighs, all the way to my knees. I stayed very still. Then, he lifted my blouse, and tried to put bills on my stomach, going up to my breasts, but my stomach was too fat, and only one of them would stay, the one covering my belly button.

"Pizza," said Pogo, smacking my stomach a little too hard.

"Look who's talking," I said. He was giving me an opening, but I was waiting for the right moment, too, and this wasn't it. I thought of what I would do. And I thought, for the thousandth time, of what he would do. Would he look at that inky printout, which resembled nothing more than a galactic cloud, an obscured thumbprint, his and mine together, and would he, like always, say just the right, wrong thing? I thought of taking that square of paper with my future printed on it and placing it over his crotch and saying, "Here. How much is this worth?"

"I thought you said I was cute," he pouted, the insult to me already forgotten.

"The Pillsbury dough boy is adorable," I said. Pogo had a round face, and he was flabby in the middle, but tall enough that he came off as sturdy and strong. Would his baby have his baby face? His cheek was smooth to the touch. I imagined a tiny hand reaching out to it. I felt something tighten inside me. When I was a kid, what did I imagine about having a baby? Why do I only remember playing with dolls that looked like little adults? What would Pogo do? How could I know him for this long and not know the answer to that?

"Nya-nya 'doughboy' nya-nya. Very funny. You're not as funny as me," he said. "I'm the funniest of all."

"You're the King of Comedy," I said. "Throw some more money at me, and I promise I'll say whatever you want to hear."

"I'm deeply, deeply wounded by your sarcasm," Pogo said sarcastically. He attempted to put a fifty over my mouth. "You promised," he said. I breathed out through my nose and the bill fluttered down to land on the floor mat. He snatched it up.

"Beautiful money," he said. "I've mistreated you." He stroked it and reinserted it in the stack he held. He collected the bills from my thighs, along with the others that had landed on the floor of the car,

40

and folded the wad back into his pocket. He leaned over the gearshift and kissed me. Slowly, he kissed all of the places where the money had been. When we were having sex, his pants were pushed down around his knees, and I could feel the bulging cash rub against my ankle.

WHEN POGO MENTIONS the cash to his brother and Natasha, Natasha emits a restrained laugh that sounds like a sigh. She drinks more slowly than the rest of us. In fact, I swear she's drinking ginger ale, but that's impossible in this crowd. She's naturally poised, the kind of woman I could hate, with legs that you'd expect to find on a tall blonde, except she isn't; she gives the illusion of tall, and she's a brunette. She has a brown bob that falls to her shoulders, and it's so perfect that when she moves her head at all, it swings. It swings and brushes her shoulders like hair in a shampoo commercial. Maybe that's why she's always tilting her head one way or the other—she knows it does that. She teaches dance aerobics, which for the men is synonymous with sexual appetite, but to me it only sounds strangely retro. The men imagine her muscle tone and flexibility. They probably imagine her doing the splits, as if you'd do that, as if aerobics is the same as cheerleading in their minds. Or I guess Cheever doesn't have to imagine it.

Natasha isn't part of their usual circle, but Pogo says her father is someone, just not the usual someone. "Someone else," I chuckle. My father is definitely not someone. Whatever her father is, Natasha doesn't quite have to work. She's deciding what to do next, while she teaches those classes. She would make a good PR person or even a newscaster for local TV. She has presence. She says she likes doing a physical job, but it's "just for now."

"Just for now," Pogo imitated her voice and the way she tilts her head and gazes wide-eyed at your face, as if you matter. This was on our way into the club, after we left Broder's.

41

"Until Cheever marries me," Pogo amended, with a pert bob of his head.

"Do you think he will?" I asked. Pogo laughed and stirred the remains of his drink with his index finger. He sucked the rum off of his finger and left the empty glass behind a potted plant in the lobby.

Natasha fits in at the club in ways that I don't. It's her confidence, and she can look like anything, like them. And Pogo laughed about his brother marrying her. This depresses me more than it should.

Then Pogo said, "If Cheever did marry her, he'd live up to his name."

"Cheever" is short for "overachiever." Their father calls him "the overachiever" and Pogo "the underachiever." I don't know Cheever's real name. Pogo's is Porter, his grandmother's maiden name. He made up the nickname. He never liked the idea of "Porter," as if he would be expected to carry things for people.

Natasha and Cheever have only been together for a few months. One morning, when they had just started dating, we were lying around at Pogo and Cheever's house, watching *The Breakfast Club* on cable. Pogo was doing all the Judd Nelson lines. I was in awe of Natasha's pajamas. They were the kind with pants and a top that had a collar and buttons. I don't think I've worn anything like that since I was ten. Her face was scrubbed so that her skin shined, and the pajamas looked as if they were pressed. I wondered how she could look that good in the morning, then I realized she probably didn't put them on until she was leaving Cheever's bedroom. She hadn't slept in them. I'd pulled on one of Pogo's T-shirts and a pair of sweatpants that were unraveling where they were cut off into shorts.

"Nice PJs." Even Pogo noticed. He can't let anything pass without a comment. He started calling her "PJ" after that, until Cheever said he had to stop because Natasha didn't want to stay over. But once Pogo knows something bothers you, you're done for. Every now and then, "PJ" slips out, and he gasps and covers his mouth, as if he just forgot.

WHEN IT'S TIME for our reservation, we're led to a small, square table covered with a white cloth in the center of the club's dining room. I half-expect a spotlight to shine on us, as each one of us takes a side. Four equal sides. Pogo sits down first, and Cheever pulls out a chair for Natasha, then sits down between them, so the two men are next to each other, and I'm next to Natasha. That's strange. Shouldn't we sit boy-girl?

Everything is dark wood. There's a giant quarry-stone fireplace on one wall and antiques all around, but the carpet is 1970s: orange fleur-de-lis, encircled by rust-brown borders in a shield pattern, all on a maroon background. I bet that seemed like a good idea at the time. Good ideas almost always become bad ideas, eventually.

Perry Como is singing above our heads. "Who's that?" says Natasha. "Harry Connick?"

"The club never plays anything newer than Bing Crosby," says Cheever.

"*Some enchanted evening . . .*" says Pogo. "*Prost!*" He raises his glass, and we all toast.

No one is paying attention to the incongruent carpet. Everyone else in the room seems full of the privilege of belonging there, which comes out not in stiff formality, but in the offhand way they talk, eat, laugh, blow their noses into the cloth napkins. They take for granted their right to be there as much as I would walking into a public library. What did they ever doubt in their lives? Of course I know they must have doubts, but at the moment it seems like I'm the only one who does. Maybe it's my whacked out hormones, but the ugly carpet makes me feel like crying. The carpet is ugly, and I still don't belong.

We're brought a menu on which there are no prices. It occurs to me that all Pogo will do at the end of the meal is sign the tab. No flash of his bundle will even be necessary. But it doesn't matter. In fact, it's the point: We know the money is there without seeing it. Pogo orders a bottle of Dom Perignon. He winks at the waiter, as if he'll agree it's a cliché. "An example of the finest in conspicuous consumption, Lovey," Pogo says, in his Thurston Howell voice. He pats my hand.

Pogo stays in character when the waiter brings the champagne. "This should keep the riff-raff at bay," he says. The waiter nods and smiles, but his smile is a business reflex; it disappears immediately.

I haven't finished my gin and tonic, so it's still in front of me, and now the champagne. I know I shouldn't be drinking. What if Pogo does "do right by me," as the doctor said? And what if that doesn't mean the same thing to Pogo, and to me, as it does to the doctor? But I'm not going to pass up Dom Perignon. I've never tried it before.

Cheever keeps squeezing Natasha's arm as if she's a fresh loaf of Wonder Bread, and each time she looks over at him with her big toothy smile, all aglow. Mayo with that? When the waiter leaves, we make all the toasts we can think of from different countries, and then we say things that just sound like toasts. "Nazdarovya!" "Salud" "Spacibo!" "Gesundheit!" "L'Chaim!" "Placebo!" "Cin-Cin!" "Chim-Chimnee!"

I sip the champagne. Now I know what people mean when they say "very dry." This champagne is very dry. I like it. Pogo has brought me to the club before, but never to the formal dining room, only to the pool and the casual bar. I feel like a kid playing dress-up, which is ridiculous, because I dress up every day for my job. I'm a professional. Just what I'm professional at is still up for discussion. But unlike Natasha, I go to work in an office where the goal is to make money, and there are demands. I spend many hours sorting through paper files, trying to find things that other people lost or misfiled. A chain of information we're following is broken; it can't be broken, it has to be one continuous line. When I find the right piece of information, people are inordinately grateful, as if I've saved their work from a burning building. My boss wants to train me to be his right hand. But if I'm his right hand, how can I ever detach myself? And where's the advancement potential? Do I eventually move up to become his brain? When I go to look for another job, how do I describe this one? I'm a finder? I can find a needle in a haystack. I'm like a dog: If you put a certain kind of dog in a swimming pool with one drop of blood, the dog will smell the blood. Or maybe I wish I were like that. Or maybe that would be too upsetting, to always smell the blood. That dog never gets a break, because where can you possibly go where there isn't at least one drop of blood? It would be like trying to get away from yourself.

I never pictured myself in this job. It's still not clear to me what the company actually does. "Investment management," whatever that means. When I finished college, I don't remember saying to myself, or to anyone, "A career in investment management!" But it's how I met Pogo. He came in one day for a meeting when I was sitting at the front desk. I looked pretty—I was wearing a long, tight skirt with a slit up the back—and he leaned over me, flirting and taking Andes mints out of the bowl. He took the green wrappers from the mints and folded them into an origami bird, and after I went back to get my boss and they went into a meeting, I noticed he had left the bird on my mouse pad with his business card. He had written: "You have beautiful feathers."

He always knows what to say to get what he wants. He never tells me I'm pretty anymore. He says I already know it. He only wants to hear that he is.

"DRINK UP," says Pogo. Cheever and Pogo are having a race.

"Boys, boys," says Natasha. "Champagne this good is meant to be savored." She takes a tiny sip. Her hair brushes her shoulder. I'm not sure whether I want to hug her or slap her.

Pogo winks at her over the rim of his glass. "Purely for medicinal purposes," he says. He throws back his head and drains the glass.

"Take it easy," says Cheever, not quite putting his glass down. The two men scowl at each other.

"Let's order," says Pogo, making like he'll pitch his empty glass into the stone fireplace. "And I'll paint a picture for you: the deal of the year."

But when the waiter comes, Cheever tells him we need a few minutes. I feel dizzy; my stomach is fluttering. Too much drink and not enough food. I try hard to focus on the menu: Signature club salad. Shrimp cocktail. Onion soup. Filet mignon. Lobster. Rack of lamb. The words are wavering, and I misread it, Signature cocktail. Lobster lamb.

"No one in the office wanted this building on their portfolio," Pogo began. "They all thought it was a real dog. But I knew better." He poured himself more champagne and held the drink up to his face, as if he was looking through the glass at me. "I knew I could make it into a show dog."

Natasha leans into Cheever and whispers in his ear. He holds her hand so that their fingers are intertwined, and I can see her French manicure. I glance down at my fingernails, rusty red, chipped polish, rimmed with paper cuts, occupational hazard. Cheever and Natasha's forearms are pressed together on the table, like Natasha just lost at arm-wrestling. Finally, Cheever raises his champagne glass, and Natasha turns her glowy grin on me. Her only facial imperfection is a slight crinkling of her nose when she smiles, leaving the impression that, although she's extremely happy, something nearby smells bad.

"Pogo. Miranda," Cheever begins. "Natasha and I have a little announcement of our own. Do you mind?" They glance meaningfully at each other, and, not waiting for Pogo to answer, Cheever gives Natasha the eyebrow signal to go ahead. Pogo's eyes half-close, and he raises his finger as if to speak, but doesn't. He has a look of indulgent irritation.

There are little squares of light on Natasha's irises, such that I can honestly describe her eyes as glittering. "We're getting married!" she says.

Her mouth is an open smile, her eyebrows are raised to full height, her nose crinkles, and she freezes like that, waiting for our response. I don't know what to say or do. For a moment, I freeze along with her. It should be me with those lit-up eyes and that wide smile. Looking at her face, a mask of manufactured joy, I can imagine her entertaining a roomful of preschoolers. And I think I've just forecast her long-term career. I exhale, not realizing that I've been holding my breath. I may throw up again, but this time I may not make it to the bathroom. I manage to squeak, "Congratulations! How wonderful!" I don't hear Pogo say anything.

Cheever kneads Natasha's hand in his. They look like game show contestants who are sure they're about to hear they've won the jackpot and are doing a poor job containing their enthusiasm in the interest of good sportsmanship. Then Cheever squeezes Natasha's bread arm again and adds to the mix: "And we're going to have a baby!"

I'm sure that all color has drained from my face.

It sounds like an afterthought, as if he'd said, "And the honeymoon will be in Bermuda!"

I develop a sudden cramp in my side; or maybe it was there all along. I clap my hands together with apparent glee to cover my speechlessness. It's too sharp and loud, and people at the next table turn to look.

Pogo does not miss a beat. He snaps his fingers. "Jeeves?" The waiter steps up. Jeeves will be spitting in our food now. "Bring these two lovebirds another bottle of champagne!"

When a second bottle of champagne is produced, it occurs to me that Pogo is trying to get a pregnant woman drunk. I'm not talking about myself. For a moment I've forgotten my own condition, more stunned by their news than by my own.

"I'm so happy for you!" I gush. "We'll have to go shopping together!" As if Natasha and I do that all the time. The truth is, if we'd known each other in high school, she never would have talked to me unless she wanted something. I fight the urge to ask Natasha how far along she is, the kind of talk two pregnant women would share; it feels too dangerous. I stand up and give her a hug, and I give Cheever a hug and a kiss on the cheek. In spite of their apparent enthusiasm, their return hugs are polite, with little actual body contact.

How did this happen? But then I see Pogo's face and I understand that it's happened to him, actually, more than anyone else at the table.

"A lot of trouble to upstage me," says Pogo, with fake jocularity. "Getting your girlfriend pregnant, that's pretty extreme. Didn't know you'd take it that far."

Sometimes I can't tell when he's only playing. If he knew the score on his side, I wonder what he'd say. I briefly entertain the idea of making my own little announcement. It's as if there are two different conversations going on, the one everyone else is having, and the imagined one in my head. I have to try hard not to confuse myself.

"Planning to finish that?" Pogo points to my glass. I shrug. He drinks the rest of my champagne. He makes a big deal about ordering lobster for all of us. "So much to celebrate!" he says.

Do I even feel like eating lobster? The smallest decision seems impossible.

"Ooh, lobster," says Natasha, twirling a strand of hair around her finger. Her poise is beginning to slip. Her glass is almost empty. Cheever refills it. This seems unwise to me.

"This will be our first lobster together," Natasha tells Cheever. "I want to remember the first everything!"

Pogo gets up from the table, agitated. His feigned good humor is giving way. His cloth napkin falls from his lap to the ground. He says, "See a man about a horse," and walks off. And leaves me alone with the moony almost-married baby-makers. I will kill him.

"So." I poke around for something to open with. As much as I'd rather talk about anything else, even aerobics, I stick with the thing I know they'll want to talk about. "Tell me about your plans." I try to sound sufficiently excited. "Is there a date?" Open to interpretation whether I'm talking about the wedding or the baby.

Before Natasha can answer, Cheever interjects, "Why don't we wait for Pogo, and then we can tell you both about it?"

Natasha frowns. "I don't mind explaining it twice," she says. "I don't mind explaining it a hundred times!"

"Of course you don't," says Cheever, with only a hint of resignation.

"We've decided to roll our wedding and honeymoon into one. We're getting married in Bermuda!"

How did I know that? And with any luck, they will disappear in the Bermuda Triangle.

"Wonderful!" I exclaim. So wonderful I can't bear the thought of continuing the conversation. "Hey—I'm really curious about your exercise class." Natasha is all ears, though I can tell I've annoyed her by not asking when the wedding will be, or say, what size gown she'll fit into by then.

"Are you inspired by Jane Fonda?"

"Fonda's old school," she says. Her smile is set, and her voice is flat, even-keeled patience. "These days what we call aerobics is really not that at all. We prefer to think of it as holistic movement." She's narrating an instructional video now. "It's integrated dance, all about being aware of your body in space. The old exercise moves put to music were so unnatural. We're all about allowing your body to do what it wants to do, and still feeling the burn."

My body in this case, is all about lying on a beach somewhere far away from Natasha. As in, not Bermuda. I feel the burn, all right.

"How do people know which way to go?" I make directional hula-type movements with my arms, as if dance aerobics includes such a maneuver. I wouldn't know. "Do most people go the right way from the beginning?"

She sighs so I know that I'm torturing her in the only way I can. I feel a little guilty, but not much. She squints in deep thought, even though, like a politician, she already knows exactly what she plans to say. I want to say, "This is a test. We are now conducting a test of the Emergency Small-Talk System."

"Yes," Natasha says. "Most people do. The people who don't get the hang of it don't come back." She looks as if she's pleased about that, but she can't help how she looks. Her eyes are light brown and large, and she has long, thick lashes. Her face is generally what would be called "sunny." Always. This must help in her job. I try to match her sunniness with a big smile of my own. I think I can do it. I can copy her. As if that's enough to make me fit. We sit there smiling big at each other, like it's a contest. I tilt my head toward my right shoulder, just like she does. If we kiss right now, we won't bump noses. But what I want is to see her not smile for once. What would do that?

"They have an amazing teacher who makes it look easy," says Cheever. He puts his arm around her and squeezes her to him, almost knocking over a water glass with his hand and dragging the white tablecloth toward him along with her body. The tremor crosses the table, and I grab Pogo's champagne glass to stabilize it. Cheever kisses Natasha's smooth hair. There's a break in her expression. It's quick; I might be wrong. But I see her eyes go sharp for a second: she didn't like it; she didn't want him to kiss her. Only on her terms, is that it?

"We're picking out rings after this!" Natasha suddenly announces, halfway freeing herself from Cheever's grip. Cheever's turn to frown and squint at his plate, as if he sees a speck that doesn't belong there. What's that about? If she only makes things *look* easy, doesn't it imply that they're actually difficult? But what do I know? I'm one of the people who wouldn't come back.

"What did I miss?" Pogo's holding a glass that's almost empty. He stopped and hung out at the bar on his way back from the bathroom. I feel my face turning red. He left me alone with them because he couldn't stand it. He didn't want to deal with them, so he just walked away. And I wonder why I was ever uncertain about how he would behave when I tell him my news. Now he stands between my chair and Natasha's. He bends down and kisses my forehead, and then he puts his hand on Natasha's back, rubs gently, right below her neck, and with his face close to hers says, "How's the bubbly, PJ?"

"Damn it, man." Cheever gets halfway up from his chair. Natasha's cheeks have gone splotchy red, and she looks at Pogo sideways, startled. She forgets to tilt her head. Pogo straightens up and walks behind me to his seat. Cheever is the bull at a bullfight after the picador sticks him. Bloodied and pissed off. Now I understand the seating arrangement: Cheever didn't want Pogo sitting next to his girlfriend.

When Pogo sits down, the waiter immediately arrives with French onion soup for everyone. "Well, la-dee-da," says Pogo. "Look at that." He must have ordered it.

I excavate the dense cheese layer with the side of my spoon and come up with a long string that won't cut. The string dangles from my mouth to the bowl. I finally pinch it apart with my fingers. And then I bite the end that's in my mouth. The thin filament, now loose, floats down like a spider's umbilical thread. This is not going the way I imagined.

Natasha begins giggling uncontrollably. I look up from my cheese string challenge to see Cheever attempting to hang a spoon from his nose. He places it carefully, but it falls to his lap. His face is red and intense and unsmiling, as if he's channeled his anger into this parlor trick. He does it again. It falls with a clatter onto the soup. The cheese layer prevents splashing. Natasha obligingly moves his plate away.

"He can do it," she says. "I've seen him," as if he's trying to leap a tall building in a single bound. But her confidence in him somehow makes me feel better.

"Cheevah, you're attracting unwanted attention." Pogo's back to Thurston Howell. Or is it William F. Buckley? I feel his hand on my leg, moving up under my skirt. I guess he doesn't want Cheever attracting my attention. Pogo can get jealous that way. I can't imagine he's truly concerned about his brother and me. But he's full of imagined slights. My anger at him dissolves.

"Wait for it; wait for it," says Cheever. With grim determination, he places the spoon once more. There must be a magical position you have to hit, because this time he gets it. He slowly draws his hands apart, ready to grab the spoon should it fall. No one says a word. Even Pogo seems to hold his breath. Only his fingers move, under the elastic of my underpants.

With his free hand, Pogo places a spoon on his own nose. He does it in only two tries. Must be a family talent. Cheever glares at him; if it's possible to look menacing with a spoon on your face, he does. Overachiever, indeed.

How Pogo can be doing what he's doing in my underwear and still keep the spoon on his nose speaks to an even greater talent for entertainment than I've given him credit for. I want him to stop. I also want him to keep going. My breath quickens.

Natasha picks up a teaspoon and tries the spoon trick herself. But her nose is too small and sharp. She gives me the signature wide-eyed, you're-important stare. "You could do it," she says. "Your nose is . . . better-shaped than mine."

The fingers are withdrawn. Pogo wipes them on the napkin that's in my lap. I'm breathing too hard. I drink a lot of water all at once.

"Come on, give it a try," says Natasha, as if she's talking to a child. Forget the spoon. I want to poke her big eyes with my fork. Yes, I'm sure I can do it better than she can. I'm sure I can make myself into a fool much better than she can.

I almost feel like crying again, because Pogo took me past the halfway point and deserted me, and because Natasha, who doesn't know me at all, wants me to put a spoon on my nose. What fucking planet am I on? I cover by sipping from my fresh glass of champagne. Maybe the bubbles will help my stomach. I want whatever is fluttering there to quiet down. Moths, sleep.

Natasha checks her watch and squeaks in delight, as if the spoons are setting some kind of record. Pogo winks at her. His spoon holds. I wonder how many girlfriends he's stolen from Cheever over the years. I wonder why I feel like hating her so much and not hating Pogo.

The waiter and a busboy are standing by with the lobster. Can they accomplish placing it in front of us without disturbing the spoon situation? They're wise enough to wait. Cheever's forehead perspires. Finally, his spoon falls, glancing off his plate with a clatter. I feel a pang of disappointment. I realize, suddenly, that I wanted Cheever to win. Or I wanted Pogo to lose.

A moment later, Pogo's spoon falls, too. It sounds like a waiter dropping things, and people turn to look. Cheever says, "I lasted the longest. I started before you." Pogo imitates him, like a child would mock another child's face when talking.

Natasha hugs Cheever's arm. "You were great," she tells him.

I want them to leave now and get their rings. Or they should get spoons. They should get married with matching spoons on their noses, engraved with lovey-dovey messages: "I'll spoon with you, forever, sweetheart."

The lobsters are delivered. My lobster is sunburned and splayed, its claws hanging over the edges of the plate, its shell glossy and forbidding. It's too complete an animal, too anatomically correct. There's no ignoring what it once was. If only I'd insisted on steak. But Pogo is trying to make it nice. And he's showing off, and lobster is inarguably celebratory. I tap the hard shell with the little fork they gave me, gently, like an egg. I have the oddest impulse to give the creature a name.

Pogo flourishes his napkin: "Nothing up my sleeve," he says. He holds up his pinky. "Ready?"

At Pogo's signal, we all begin to eat. And he begins to talk. In between large buttery bites of lobster, he tells the story of his deal, as if he was never interrupted, as if there's no big news besides his own. He paints every detail for us. We're supposed to savor it, along with the meal.

Of course, I've heard it before. Natasha is rapt. She cracks open a claw, but then seems to forget it's there. She holds onto it, her lips moist. At the mention of Pogo's commission, which is substantially more than what he has in his pocket, she says, "That's for one deal alone?"

"He gets a deal like that two, maybe three times a year, if he's lucky," Cheever says. Natasha doesn't look at him.

"You must be really good at what you do," she says to Pogo.

"As good as any of us," says Cheever.

"Why thank you," says Pogo. He holds his lobster's claws in the air and attempts to click them together. "How do you like my castanets?" he asks. He swallows the last of his champagne, and then he sings: "*La cucaracha, la cucaracha*."

I can't take anymore. I feel a tight ball of anger thickening inside me, as if to feed what grows there. Soon there will be room for nothing else. I'm ready to make a big deal out of something. Out of nothing. I want to test Pogo, just to see what will happen, to see if he'll fight me here, if I can get him to fight me here, in the middle of the club, in the midst of his overshadowed glory, over something that doesn't matter at all. "That's a Mexican song," I say "Castanets are from Spain."

"And the Pope is from Poland," says Pogo.

"No one in Spain would sing that song."

"We're not in Spain," says Pogo. "And you're not Spanish."

"I minored in Spanish."

"Minor, shminor. Don't worry your pretty head," says Pogo. "So we stood in the lobby, and I showed her—"

He goes on with his story. I want to make him ridiculous, but I can't, because he won't even fight me. He's dismissed me. And there's a giant bug on my plate. Was it human when it went to sleep last night? Did it awaken to find itself forever changed? Like me, I catch myself thinking. Mutant.

I can't bring myself to eat it. The smell of the hot butter, the dark stew of the onions in the soup, the salty steam coming off the lobster, it's all too much. The moths will not subside.

Cheever notices: "Is there something wrong with your lobster?" He seems genuinely concerned.

"Yes, I think so."

The tail, the way it curls, I can see in it an embryo, approximately eight weeks in development. It does not, at this point, look human. They say it can remind you of a shrimp. Here, if a shrimp grew big and hard and red and landed on my plate—a lobster. Here it is, and it will not go away so easily. It will only continue to grow like this: now what will you do?

The printout of the sonogram is still in my purse. My big night happened eight weeks ago. I just didn't know it at the time. I don't say any of this.

"I'm not very hungry." I do say that. "Would you like my tail?" I ask Natasha.

"Oh, I couldn't, I'm stuffed," she says.

"You don't want your tail?" says Pogo.

"No—take it," I say. He takes it.

"Do you want your tail?" he asks Natasha.

"I've eaten some," she says. "Would you like the rest?"

"Yes, I would like the rest of your tail," Pogo says.

"Goddamn it." Cheever slams his fist down on the table. "It's not funny."

"I don't know what you mean," says Pogo, aiming a commiserating grin first at Natasha and then at me.

It happened the night he accused me of cheating. He went into one of his rages that are so baseless I always think he's faking just for the melodrama. He insisted I'd gone off into a room with another man at a party. We were on the rug that half-covered the parquet floor in my bedroom when he made this accusation.

I was like a foal, new and licked clean a moment before. He had kissed down my belly, and now his head was between my thighs, and I was propped up on one elbow, watching him. He stopped, but didn't lift his head. I put my hand on his thick, black hair. I held onto it tightly, but resisted the urge to press his head down into me. Instead, he escaped my grip and yanked my underwear from around my ankle. He held my panties aloft, up to the light, looking for proof, as if he'd see another man's sperm there. He stood over me naked and erect, his bangs flopped over one eye. I stared at his penis.

"You two were gone for a long time." He said it calmly. I knew what was coming next, and it wasn't me. "You two-timing slut. You cunt. This proves it. He was in your pants." He wouldn't hear me, of course. My "That's crazy; *you* were in my pants," and "I'm not interested in him. Why would I do that?"

It took me a while to figure out that Pogo attributes to me everything that he does himself. The other women. He assumes I'm like him.

I moved away from him, scooting sideways on the rug, like a crab. He tossed the underwear in my face. He walked out and slammed the door.

An hour later he shouted to me from outside, below my window. "Are you awake?" he called. "I'm sorry. Can I come in?"

"WHAT ABOUT the claw?" says Pogo. "Are you leaving the claw, too?"

"Have at it," I say. "Excuse me." I get up to go to the bathroom.

To my great annoyance, Natasha pops out of her chair and says, "I'll go, too!" And in a lower voice, she adds, "I have to go all the time, now, if you know what I mean." I glance immediately at her waist, where her tailored blouse tucks into her fitted skirt. She's not showing yet. And off we go, the best of friends now, with "Meet Me in the Ladies' Room" playing on the soundtrack in my head.

The black woman is still there. She's inside a stall with the door open, and her wide back is toward me. She wipes the chrome paper dispenser, the flush handle, the door handle. She sprays some cleaner and wipes things with a rag. I note with some distaste that she's using the same rag for everything. I wonder if the gold fleur-de-lis is printed on it.

Natasha talks loudly to me, and laughs. "It's so hard to hold it when I'm teaching the dance class. I might have to give it up soon." She glances in the mirror at her teeth. "Don't say anything, okay? I haven't told Cheever yet." She goes into the stall and keeps talking to me. "What do men know about being pregnant? It's like my bladder shrank to pea size! My bladder shrinks, while I get fat! I keep asking myself, what else can happen?"

What else? You can have a baby, nitwit. She could say the same thing to me.

"My friends with babies are telling me, take the drugs, Nat. But I don't know. Pioneer women didn't have the benefit of epidurals."

And half of them died in childbirth, probably, Nat, I feel like saying. She babbles on and on. She only needs me here so she can pretend she isn't talking to herself. I wonder if she notices the attendant. When I left the table, I thought I was going to throw up again, but now that I'm here, I realize I won't. Maybe it was enough to get away from the smell of the lobster. I go into a stall and wonder if I'll be able to pee while Natasha's still talking to me. I have a shy bladder. I have a cramp in my side from holding it in.

I sit and wait. Natasha keeps talking. "The wedding's going to be at the Princess. It's the nicest hotel on the island. It'll be small, because how many people will fly to Bermuda? Oh, maybe everyone! But it'll be so elegant."

I'm trying to make her words into white noise. She doesn't seem to require answers. While I sit, I take the square paper out of my purse. It's a shrimp, a crustacean, a galactic cloud, a fingerprint, a mass, a nothing. Besides my doctor, I'm the only person in the world who knows of its existence. I suddenly feel that, and feel it fiercely, like a hand around my throat. I struggle for air. I lean back against the tank, waiting for the feeling to pass. I stay that way for a while.

There's a flush. "Miranda, are you in there?" Natasha is back at the mirror. I tell her yes. I force myself to get up.

I stand next to Natasha at the mirror. The attendant moves around behind me. She's going in and out of the stalls that each of us vacated; I notice abstractly, but don't really pay attention. I put on lipstick, while Natasha fixes her hair.

"You'll come to Bermuda, won't you?" She's Ms. Magnanimous now. I feel a touch evil.

"Will you be giving birth there, as well?" I ask.

She stares at me, silent, and then laughs, "Oh you're so funny! You said it so seriously, at first I thought, you know . . ."

In the mirror, I see the attendant glance up from her cleaning. Natasha puts her towel in the basket and walks out. Behind her, I move to do the same, but my hands are shaking, and I drop it on the floor. I reach for it, but the woman bends faster, grabs it up, and puts it away for me. As I straighten up, I meet her eyes and hold her look for a moment. She does her best to stay bland, but I can see she knows my secret. She has cleaned it up for me. The only other person on earth.

I STAND AT the entrance to the dining room, and I watch them from a distance, from across the heads of the other diners. They're animated. Pogo's hands are cutting the air; Natasha's movements are small and neat, her head turning toward one man and then the other. I see the layout of the room, the pattern of the tables, the

Rorschach of the carpet. The song from earlier is back, repeating: *Some enchanted evening . . .*

Natasha gives a little wave. Cheever stands, and Pogo leans over and kisses me on the mouth. I sit and look at my plate. My lobster is an empty shell; they've all taken parts of it, like I said they could. I put my hand in Pogo's lap and find the place where he's still warm.

DUBROVNIK 1989

WHEN HIS GIRLFRIEND rang the doorbell, he told me to hide in the bathroom. Mildew on the cinderblock walls; wet towel on the floor; beard stubble, like metal shavings, in the sink. He wore a goatee. I thought it was funny that he went to the trouble to maintain a goatee but didn't flush the toilet. But, look, he lived alone. He hadn't been expecting me. We'd gone off for a beer that became two, and then shared a joint in the park before I ever saw the inside of his place.

He was a Vietnam vet and lived in an English basement where he repaired electronics for people. I met him when I brought my VCR to be fixed. There was an entryway inside the front door with a curtain that hid his living space from view. He'd open the front door, you'd step into the hall and hand him whatever was broken. He'd take it and disappear behind the curtain and then come back with a receipt. My VCR was jammed; there was a tape stuck inside that wouldn't eject. *Fatal Attraction*. I'd tried to extract it myself first. There was something I loved about the process of taking things apart and examining their innards. Maybe it came from watching my father try to fix things—a broken socket, a clogged carbure-tor. I unscrewed the VCR's casing, and I could see the video, but I couldn't get to it; it was in the grip of a steel trap, tape wound around spindles, paralyzed.

There were clothes and gadgets and tools scattered around the room. From his bed, I could see the pile of VCRs stacked in one corner, with a sweater tossed on top. Mine was under the sweater.

He said the woman at the door was his *ex*-girlfriend, and she wanted money. He sent her away.

In bed, he put a handful of my hair in my mouth like a gag and said, "Should I fuck you now?" and I nodded, because I couldn't speak with my hair like that.

There was a Marine Corps tattoo on his bicep and a green dragon on his chest. One of his nipples was the dragon's nostril. The dragon seemed unoriginal—I mean, a dragon must be number three on the list of most common tattoos, after a skull and a rose—but he had a good body with only the early signs of a beer gut. I tried to shut my eyes to the room and just feel his body. He smelled like Listerine or something else minty with alcohol in it; maybe it was his shaving cream. His skin was clammy. I didn't have enough time to come, and then he did, and that was it. That was annoying. And then he lay next to me and told me his ex-girlfriend was a heroin addict, but that he'd been tested recently and he was negative. I didn't say any-thing, because I was frozen with horror.

"Don't worry," he said, without looking at my face. "Unless you want to."

Then he acted bored and ignored me until I said, "I'm leaving," and he said, "Bye," and I left.

THAT HAD TO be the lowest I'd sunk. That's what I thought, I'd finally hit bottom. I didn't go back, not even to get my VCR, even though he left me a message a few days later saying it was ready. I thought of Glenn Close, from the movie: *I'm not going to be ignored*.

I didn't have a boyfriend at the time. I was sleeping with men who didn't want to be boyfriends. Lucas and I had conversations about this, about whether women could sleep with people and not care. It had started to feel like a challenge. I didn't tell Lucas about the VCR guy, because in that case I seemed to have failed the challenge. I told him almost everything else, and he told me what seemed like almost everything.

Lucas was the kind of friend you could spend an intense twelve hours with the first time you met and then feel like you knew each other completely. In fact that's exactly what had happened. We were both working at an event his boss had catered, and my boss, an event planner, had organized. That was last fall, when I'd only been in the job for a couple of months. Lucas was a banquet waiter. It was a fancy party, and he was wearing a tux, and I was wearing a long dress, and he kept bringing me canapés, even though he knew I wasn't a guest. In a fake, mincey voice, he'd say, "Would you care for a *vol-au-vent*—that is, one of our petit pastry shells stuffed with escargot and *beurre à l'ail avec chapeau de champignon*?"

When everyone else had gone home, after I made sure the table-cloths I'd ordered were set aside to be returned to the rental company, and Lucas was finished packing up dishes and glassware, we got drunk together on the open booze that couldn't be returned to the liquor supplier. We talked until four in the morning and he never laid a hand on me. This was a welcome novelty, because that night at least, I felt like I needed a break from hands and mouths and everything else. I told him I didn't want a boyfriend for a while. I needed to be okay with just me, by myself. I needed to look inside instead of outside for contentment. I sounded like a self-help book, but he didn't laugh at me.

Still, some things were too humiliating even to tell Lucas.

I DID TELL him about Gray, who came after VCR-guy.

When Gray introduced himself, saying, "I'm Gray," I'd tried not to laugh. His hair was silver; his eyes were gray-blue.

"I'm Miranda Weber," I said. I wasn't sure then if Gray was his first or his last name, so I gave him both of mine.

"You're here every morning, Miranda Weber," he said.

So are you, I should have said. But I just blushed because he'd noticed.

I'd developed the habit of sitting in the generic café near my office before work. I drank black coffee and ate a cup of peach yogurt and a plain bagel. I'd started this about a month earlier, when eating breakfast at home became unbearable. I had no food in my apartment to speak of; I didn't like to eat there with my roommate and her fisheye. When I first moved in, she liked me; then she tolerated me; now she was openly hostile. The last time I saw her in daylight, she was dividing the living room in half with a line of masking tape.

"This is your half," she said. Her half had the TV.

The bagels in the café were bland and spongy, but comforting, like chewing on my pillow. I'd sit there thinking and reading the newspaper and eavesdropping, and unconsciously tear off pieces of bagel, rolling them into pebble-size balls between my fingers before popping them into my mouth.

Gray was always there with the same woman. She wore boxy skirt-suits and blouses buttoned to the neck. They drank coffee and had what seemed like a lively conversation. He was probably in his mid-fifties. He looked old to me, and distinguished, like he had an important job and some money. His life, I imagined, was a magazine ad for Johnny Walker: at home he'd put on a pair of worn leather slippers and sit in a big leather chair by a fire in a room that was painted forest green, with a built-in shelf of old books behind him, a globe on the desk, and an Irish setter at his feet.

AFTER SOME WEEKS, I mostly gave up trying to hear what he and the woman were talking about, and then one morning he showed up without her, walked directly to my table and said, "Is this seat taken?"

He asked me a lot of questions. What was my job? What had I studied in college? What were my goals? It was like an interview. In fact, I thought it might be an interview, so I answered accordingly.

And then he said, "You're not married?"

I said, "No."

He said, "Boyfriend?"

I said, "Not at the moment."

"I'm married," he said. He wore a gold signet ring on his middle finger.

"To the woman who's usually here with you?" I said. I think that was the first question I asked him.

He looked puzzled for a second and then his eyes went wide, and he said, "Hell, no! That old bag?" He laughed so hard he had to wipe his eyes with a cotton handkerchief he kept in his suit coat. "'Course, my wife's an old bag, too," he said. "I call her S.T. Know what that stands for?"

"No," I said.

"Saggy tits," he said, and then laughed some more.

It was the second time in as many weeks that a man had managed to shock me. I glanced down automatically at my own chest, where my blouse was unbuttoned just enough. When I looked up again quickly, he was looking there, too.

"You don't have anything to worry about," he said. "How old are you?"

"Twenty-three," I told him.

"Do you know where I work?" he said.

"No," I said.

"Over there." He pointed out the glass front of the café toward the building across the street. "*The Washington Post*," he said.

I was impressed. I'd watched *All the President's Men* a few months before my VCR broke. I liked the part where Woodward tells Bernstein, *I don't mind what you did. I mind the way you did it.*

"That must be interesting," I said. "Are you a reporter?" He didn't look like a reporter. He wasn't rumpled.

"No, I'm on the executive side," he said. "Would you like to work there?"

"Sure," I said. My father had laminated the famous front page that said "Nixon Resigns," and hung it on the wall in my parents' bedroom. If I wanted to impress them, a job at the *Post* would do it. They'd been markedly less than impressed with me of late, even though they didn't know the half of what they could be unimpressed with.

What was most disappointing to them was my reluctance to spend time with my sister. When Donna was having one of her periodic "fits," as my mother called it, she seemed to want nothing more than to stay at home and sleep late and watch soap operas. For reasons I resisted understanding, she was willing to go places with me, even when she resisted everyone else. Blood should bypass the obstacles; I should have been trying harder to be a good sister. I should have been taking her to the movies. When she wasn't holed up in her room, she loved to go to the movies, she only didn't love to stay at the movies. I never knew what scene would upset her and make her stand up in the middle and walk out. At least I'd learned to always sit on the aisle. Still, she'd beg to go, as if the fantasy of another life was what attracted her, until she'd suddenly become aware that it was all a lie. She'd rail at the characters and their faulty logic.

"That's so stupid," she'd say. "Why would he go so close to the robot, when we could all see it wasn't dead yet?"

When I took her to see *Big*, she lasted until thirty minutes before the end. I never saw the part where Tom Hanks changes back into a little boy again. When we reached the parking lot, I drove off without my sister. I circled the block four times. Each time I passed, she was standing there faithfully, on the sidewalk in front of the Uptown, with a cheerful expression on her face, certain I'd eventually stop for her. Then I drove her home and, like every time before, my parents tried to reimburse me for the tickets, and I felt bad and said no. I should have let them, because I was waiting for all those movies to come out on tape, and now I'd also have to wait until I could afford to buy a new VCR.

In *Rain Man*, which I didn't take Donna to see, a brother's hard heart is opened to his autistic brother, an "idiot savant," after the autistic brother wins big in Vegas. Suddenly everyone wanted to have a savant for a sibling. On the few occasions I was out with Donna since that movie became popular, people looked at us differently, as if she might be a genius. Except she wasn't. Her IQ was well below average. She was no good at counting money, much less counting cards.

"If the movie doesn't work out for you," my mother had said, "why not take Donna to lunch? She loves to go out to eat."

That wasn't true; she loved McDonald's. Every family dinner out began with a stop at the drive-through window, because she refused to eat food from any other restaurant. Blood or no blood, I couldn't manage to guilt myself into these encounters often enough to please my parents. They spent much of their time and energy smoothing Donna's path through life, and my resistance was remarkable and incomprehensible to them. When I was in their house, their disappointment was like a lingering odor. The best idea, from my perspective, was to stay away.

"I HAVE TO get to work," Gray said. "And you too, yes?"

"Yes," I said.

"We can continue this conversation," he said, standing, and joggling the waistband of his trousers.

"Sure," I said.

"Over dinner," he said, which sounded only half like a question.

"Okay," I said. I followed him out of the café with my coffee in one hand and the newspaper folded under my arm like a professional.

He pointed toward K Street. "The Guards," he said.

WHEN I ARRIVED at the restaurant on the appointed night, he was already in a booth, with a martini and a cigarette. He ordered me a drink and said, "Do you like fish?"

I said yes.

"It's very good here," he said. "They fly it in from New England."

"As long as it's not from the Potomac," I said. He smiled. His face was just the right shape, a stern-jawed rectangle. The hollows of his cheeks were pitted from long-ago acne, but he was nice looking.

"Do you mind if I smoke?" he said, though he was already smoking, Benson and Hedges.

"No it's fine," I said.

"You don't smoke, do you?"

"No," I said. I didn't want to tell him that I smoked sometimes, and that the smell of his cigarette was making me want one.

The Guards was dimly lit, with brass sconces set in velvety red walls. There were white tablecloths to the floor and no prices on my menu. It felt like a place in a movie, exactly the kind of place where a man would bring a woman who's not his wife.

I was quiet because I wasn't sure how to behave. Of course I knew how to behave on a date, but I wasn't sure if Gray wanted to be my lover, my mentor, or both.

For dessert, he suggested the chocolate mousse. When it came, he asked if he could feed it to me.

"Sure," I said. I don't know if I was more taken with him or with the attention he was paying me.

He spooned a dainty portion of chocolate into my mouth and watched me carefully as I ate. His staring made me self-conscious about my manners. I dabbed at the corners of my mouth with the napkin. The confection dissolved on my tongue; at first sweet, it left a bitter aftertaste.

"I can imagine," he said, "what it feels like to be that chocolate."

LATER THAT WEEK when I had dinner with Lucas, I told him about the dinner with Gray. How he looked at me and what we ordered and how I eventually took a couple of drags from his cigarette, leaving my lipstick on the end. I didn't tell him about the chocolate mousse or how, after we left The Guards, Gray led me into an alley a half-block away, pressed me up against the bricks and put his tongue in my mouth. He tasted like green olives. He put his hand under my skirt, and I felt him fumbling around the breathable cotton crotch of my pantyhose and then moving to the waistband, but he couldn't maneuver his hand inside the pantyhose or take them down without unzipping my skirt, so he gave that up.

"Touch me," he said. He raked his tongue over my ear, and it sounded like someone fumbling with a microphone when they don't know it's switched on.

I moved my hand down his shirt, along his trim enough waist, to his hip, to his belt, and I could feel his cock against my stomach, and I was about to put my hand on his zipper, but then I didn't. I kept my hand just above his belt while I thought of all the men I'd touched there, and I couldn't do it.

So if that meant no job at the *Post*, that's what it would mean.

"I can't," I said. "First date," I added. I waited for him to get angry.

He licked my neck, and his tongue went in my mouth and out again, and he said, "You are delicious." Then he stopped and took a step back and straightened his tie, tucked in his shirt, cocked his head at me and tugged my skirt back into alignment. He looked at his watch. "We should go," he said. "I need to get home."

"Thank you for dinner," I said.

"Thank *you*," he said.

He hailed a cab and when it pulled over, he opened the door and helped me inside and handed the driver some money. He winked at me before he shut the door.

➜

My apartment building was a modest brick mid-rise, remarkable only for its location across the street from the new Soviet Embassy compound. It was like living in a shack outside the walls of Emerald City. The Soviets had been allowed to build their embassy on the highest hill in Washington. Only the National Cathedral had a better vantage point for spying. The embassy was currently unoccupied, because of all the bugs found in the walls of the new American embassy that was under construction in Moscow. Our embassy had to be torn out and rebuilt, and until it was done, bug-free, the Soviets were barred from occupying theirs. Even so, it was "monitored" twenty-four hours a day by men with coiled wires trailing out of their ears. Secret Service, they told me when I asked. I saw them whenever I came and went, including that night, when I got out of the cab under the security lights at my building's entrance. They waved.

IN MY APARTMENT, I could hear my roommate snoring. I locked myself in my room, like I might change into a werewolf and I couldn't be trusted to stay in for the night. It was early spring, and my room was cold because I'd left the bathroom window open that morning to let the steam out from the shower. Otherwise the moisture built up and made the paint peel on the ceiling. It was a casement window, and when I went to crank it shut, I saw that some birds had started to build a nest on the exterior stone ledge. I could have opened the screen and knocked the nest off the ledge before they had a chance to finish it, and then I'd be able to close my window. But I didn't. I wouldn't. I pulled on a sweater over my nightgown and went to sleep.

ON THURSDAY MORNING, Gray nodded at me when he and his colleague passed my table. When it was time to go to work, and I got up to leave, he called me over.

"I'd like you to meet Ellen," he said.

Ellen shook my hand and grinned politely as if she had no idea where my hand had almost gone nine hours before. "Gray told me about your job search," she said. "How fast can you type?"

I didn't want to be a secretary, and my education overqualified me. But I knew you wanted to get in on the ground floor, hang on by your fingernails and pull yourself up from there. I also knew that forty words per minute, my typing speed, was inadequate. So I said, "How fast would you like me to type?"

"That's the spirit," said Ellen. "Sixty words per minute should do it."

"Okay," I said.

She handed me her business card. I didn't look at it until I was at work. She was an "Executive Administrator."

I PRACTICED TYPING on the Radio Shack Trash-80 I used at Madeline's office and tested myself. Forty-five. A monkey could type faster than me.

Madeline called me into her office, frantic. She was always frantic when she wasn't in front of a client.

"How can I help?" I said. I always said that.

"I can't find my Valium," she said. She slammed her desk drawer. The pens and coins and binder clips rattled against the metal. "Would you find it for me?"

I found it for her. She didn't know how good I was at finding drugs in general.

MADELINE HAD LANDED a contract that meant she could afford a full-time assistant, but only for one year. I took the job because the friend who introduced us told me that Madeline knew a lot of people. And because I was running out of money and didn't want to ask my parents for help. They kept telling me to apply to the government. I'd filled out the interminable SF-171 employment form, but if there was one thing you learned from growing up in D.C., it was that government workers were lazy bums, and their jobs were regimented and dull as the Agriculture building, which was modeled after a prison. The desirable jobs went to people who were brought in from out of town, hired by congressmen or appointed by cabinet officials. Working for Madeline wasn't bad, even if I didn't aspire to be a meeting planner. What did I aspire to be?

"I'm a Type A personality," she said when she hired me. "You seem like a Type B personality. You can help me calm down."

Type B sounded like an assessment that would give my parents a fresh reason for disappointment. I was supposed to be "A" all the way. At work, I was; I was a conscientious employee. I was never late, and I never called in sick. It was in every other category that I was lacking.

Madeline thought she was teaching me valuable life lessons while stomping around the office suite, tossing papers this way and that, something always going wrong despite her best efforts.

"You must behave as if you anticipated it," she said, "a minor difficulty, easily solved. In private, you tear your hair out. That's called being a professional."

FRIDAY NIGHT, Lucas and I had dinner at our favorite place. It was probably our favorite only because it was rarely open. When it was closed, no explanation was ever provided, not even a hastily scrawled note taped to the door. When it was open, it seemed imperative to go. It was in a fashionable but edgy neighborhood where you could get a good meal and hear good music and get beaten up for looking the wrong way at someone all in the same two-block radius. But the latter was hardly remarkable in a city the newspapers had started calling the Murder Capital. A couple of months before, on Valentine's Day, there had been thirteen shootings in twenty-four hours.

Entering that restaurant was like entering a Middle Eastern version of *Brigadoon*. We sat on cushions on the floor among tasseled pillows that were embedded with rows of thumbnail-size mirrors. You didn't recline on them so much as gaze at your broken self.

The restaurant's owner was also the chef and the waiter. He wore an old aviator hat that he never removed, the kind with ear flaps. He stood over us and told us what to order, as if he had to leave and we were holding him up.

"Tonight," he said, "you will have the couscous." And then he disappeared behind a curtained wall. He didn't come back for a long time, but we drank mai tais and forgot about him. All you could ever get was the couscous, which was nevertheless so good, in its gravy of indeterminate yet perfectly slow-roasted meat with fragrant spices, we didn't mind that there was nothing else.

After I told Lucas about Gray and Ellen and typing, he said, "Your job ends in June. It's perfect."

"Only if I get it," I said.

"Not the *Post*," he said. "July. Dubrovnik."

We'd talked about going to Dubrovnik sometime. He was always bringing it up, as if it was the one thing he looked forward to, like Disneyland.

"I don't know if I'll have the money by then," I said. Meaning, I absolutely won't have the money by then. "I can't even afford a new VCR right now."

"I thought you were getting the old one fixed," he said.

"That didn't work out," I said.

"Maybe we shouldn't be eating here," said Lucas. "It's not cheap."

"Okay," I said. "Next time, I'll eat that burrito that's been in my freezer for three months."

"Let me pay this time," he said. "Buy me a drink when we get to Heaven." Heaven was a bar down the block. It was on the roof of a building; in the basement was Hell.

"Okay," I said. "I'll meet you there."

He scowled at me. "Why?" he said. But he knew the answer. I was stopping at Remy's first.

"Well," I said.

"If you didn't do that," he said, "you'd have had the money for Dubrovnik months ago."

I didn't answer. He tapped his fork on the table like it was a gavel.

"I'm sorry," I said.

"Forgive yourself," he said. And then, "I'd go with you if you wanted."

"Remy doesn't like people to bring friends," I said.

"I mean a meeting," said Lucas. "I'd go to a meeting."

"Christ," I said. "I'm not an addict."

"You might be depressed," he said.

"Who isn't?" I said.

"You could talk to someone," he said.

"You," I said.

He took my hand and kissed the back of it. "You have good reasons," he said.

He was talking about the abortion. It was before we met, but I'd told him about it. About the girls in the cots in recovery, with no curtains hiding us from each other. They were all whimpering or moaning. One of them, her mother was braiding her hair. One of them was sucking her thumb. I was the only white girl. I went to a clinic in a part of town where no one would know me. I lay there in that room afterward not making a sound, trying to see how long I could be silent.

After that, I'd left my boyfriend, and I'd stopped showing up to work. They fired me, "with regret."

"You have promise," my boss had said. "Get your act together," he'd said.

That's why I was eager and grateful when Madeline offered me the job, even though it was only for a year. A year had seemed like forever. I had credit card debt and student loans, and after rent and paying those down little by little, there was almost nothing left. Dubrovnik, at $750 just for the plane ticket, might as well have been the moon. So maybe I was using what little disposable income I had for a short-lived escape from all of that. A Dubrovnik of the mind.

"You need to get out of D.C.," said Lucas.

"I have," I said. "I went to Spain. In college," even though I knew that wasn't what he meant.

"You are done." The owner had appeared at our table, holding the check in front of our noses. "Who's going to pay?"

"Can we split it?" I said.

"I don't care what you do," said the owner. "One check."

Lucas plucked it from his hand.

➔

Remy's apartment always looked as if someone had either just moved in or was about to move out. There was a card table and chairs, a glass coffee table and a sofa, a TV stand and a stereo. There were no pictures on the walls, there was no rug, no knickknacks, unless you counted the scale in the center of the coffee table.

Frequent foot traffic made the neighbors suspicious, so there was the ritual to follow: greeting, glass of wine, chatting in which Remy pretended to be fascinated by everything I had to say; and testing the product, like free samples in the cheese aisle. Remy cut his powder with benzene, which smelled like cotton candy. When I snorted it, it stabbed my sinus like an ice pick, like the first breath of cold air on a freezing winter morning. After that, a dramatic demonstration of weighing, cutting, and packaging. I was never talented with origami, and the tiny packets in which Remy distributed the goods were small miracles of folding technique.

Remy had gone to do something in the kitchen. I sat on the couch drinking wine and doing lines, per his instructions. The phone rang.

"Should I get it?" a woman's voice called from what must have been the bedroom. I'd had no idea there was anyone else in the apartment.

"No," Remy shouted from the kitchen, as if he'd answered the question a million times. "Come meet my friend," he said.

A woman in a flowered silk bathrobe emerged from the bedroom. Her face was puffy and yellow. She was heavy and maneuvered carefully in the narrow space between the couch and the coffee table to sit next to me. Any jostling would have disturbed the mathematical perfection of the samples Remy had left on the table.

"How do you do?" She reached out to shake my hand and in doing so released her grip on the folds of her robe, which fell open. She was naked. She didn't seem to notice. Her breasts looked like sea lions flopped on the boulder of her belly, where the skin was stretched tight. I guessed she was in her third trimester.

She asked me to pour her some wine, but "only a drop." When she took the glass, I saw the cluster of circular burns on the inside of her wrist. She stood, and this time she held the robe closed with her free hand. Then she disappeared into the kitchen.

Why was she so pregnant? Why hadn't she done something about it while she could? She had a better reason than I'd had to not have a baby.

I did another line. It made me think of the thin brown line that ran from her navel to her bush. I didn't get far enough into my pregnancy to develop one of those, a longitude line marked in the flesh.

My packet was on the coffee table, but I hadn't paid yet. It was surprising for a coke dealer to be so trusting, to leave me alone for so long, but on the other hand, I wouldn't have wanted to cross him. When I walked into the kitchen, Remy was spooning liquid from a pot on the stove, and then heating the spoon with a small torch, the kind I'd seen Lucas use to brown crème brulée. He didn't seem to notice I was standing there. While he held the flame under the spoon, he inhaled the smoke, sucking it all in with thorough and ravenous intensity like a person in a pie-eating contest. I thought of Richard Pryor. Remy might have burned up thousands of dollars worth of blow while I was in the next room. His girlfriend took the spoon from his hand. She spilled some.

"Stupid cunt," said Remy. Then he noticed me.

"I have to go," I said. "I'll leave it on the coffee table." Meaning, the money.

"Leave it here," he said, pointing at the countertop with the torch.

I did. Then I took the delicate isosceles triangle he'd made for me and left.

To get to Heaven, you had to enter through Hell and walk up a narrow, dark staircase to the roof. I almost didn't notice the man coming toward me with the iguana on his shoulder until he was squeezing by me on the stairs, on his way down. Even though I got a close-up of its dragon face, I wasn't sure if I was really seeing it. I was wired.

Lucas was at the bar talking to two girls; one of them was very pretty, the other was the obligatory less-pretty friend. I named them Janet and Chrissy. Chrissy was the pretty one, like on *Three's Company*. Girls liked Lucas. He looked like one of the singers from Duran Duran. He was tall and on the thin side, with short dark hair and no sideburns, and a few auburn highlights, which he said were real, but I didn't believe him. I also thought he plucked his eyebrows a little; they were too neat for my taste.

"Did you see a guy with an iguana?" I said.

"I thought that was a Komodo dragon," said Chrissy.

"Those are deadly," said Lucas.

"No wonder they made him leave," said Chrissy.

"They told him to go to Hell?" I said.

Lucas laughed and the girl laughed a second later. Janet looked bored. I had that skin-crawly feeling. I had to move around or talk or something. There was dancing in Heaven, but not in Hell.

"Depeche Mode?" I said. "Let's dance." Lucas was usually willing to dance. Sometimes we went to Dart, the cavernous gay club near the Navy Yard. I liked to go there, because the men always wanted to dance, even with me. My theory was that if they weren't already dancing with a man, dancing with me at least got them some attention. Usually someone would cut in. And Lucas liked it because he was gay. Although he hadn't admitted this to me, we both understood it.

No one made a move to the dance floor. I ordered a drink from

Spencer, the bartender. Spencer looked like a wrestler, that solid, stocky build; I could see him in the kooky leotard. His tie was tucked into his shirt so it wouldn't sweep the bar when he leaned over to talk to me, and his sleeves were rolled up to expose his muscular forearms.

"He's getting some action," said Spencer. "If he wants it." Ugly smirk.

"My father's an astronaut," Lucas was saying, when I came back with my drink.

"Really?" said Janet. "Has he been to space?"

Which wasn't a dumb question, even though her friend said, "Duh."

"Not all astronauts get to go," said Lucas. "Mine did, though."

"That's amazing," said Chrissy. "Did he walk on the moon?"

"Yes," said Lucas. "Not with Neil Armstrong, though."

"Let's dance," said Chrissy. As if I hadn't already said it. She took Lucas's hand.

I was kind of glad they walked away, because I didn't know how long I could keep a straight face about the astronaut story. Lucas's father was a lawyer for the catering company where Lucas was a waiter. Lucas was always making up stories like that. Last time it happened was when we were at Dart, and he told a guy he wanted to impress that his father had been held hostage in Iran.

"What a story," the man said. Exactly what I'd been thinking.

"Yeah," said Lucas. "He never got over it. He always looks behind him when he's in a room by himself. He jumps at sudden noises, that kind of thing."

After we left, Lucas told me, "The truth is boring. My father's a lawyer," he said. "Everyone in Washington's a lawyer."

"So why not tell them your father was a famous astronaut?" I'd actually said that.

"Where's your boyfriend?" said Spencer. He meant Lucas. Lucas had said Spencer had a crush on me, but I thought Lucas had a crush on him.

The Romeo Void song was playing, and Spencer mouthed the chorus to me, gesticulating with his soda sprayer like it was a microphone and doing little pelvic thrusts that I couldn't quite see from my side of the bar. *I might like you better if we slept together / But there's something in your eyes that says maybe that's never / Never say never.*

Janet was enjoying Spencer's performance. Maybe she thought it was for her. She swayed with the music, and then leaned up against the bar, resting her chest on top of the wet wood. She asked for another drink.

The dance floor was crowded for once, and I didn't see Lucas anywhere. I went to the ladies' room.

The stalls were made of wood and painted deep blue with silver stars scattered around and graffiti etched with ballpoint pens and knives, cutting across the grain. I put Remy's art project on the ledge created by the toilet paper dispenser. I unwrapped it carefully. The powder was pink-tinged and glistened like mica. I did a bump off the stiff corner of my credit card, and then another, the familiar sweet smell. I imagined I could feel it entering my brain, finding a space there. A couple more and everything would seem clear. I leaned over, did a last one, and then one more for good luck, and I was straightening up, about to close up the paper, when the stall door opened and there was Janet staring at me, her mouth an *O* of surprise that became an evil grin. She turned and ran away. And then I was in hell.

"Shit," I told myself. "Shit. Shit. Shit," I said to the painted ceiling and the constellation Pegasus, which I began to think was incorrectly laid out and that I could do it better, that maybe my artistic skills were latent and I should take a class, maybe enroll in art school and also study astronomy in my free time, and then I could surely improve on this—I snapped out of it long enough to leave the bathroom, return to the bar, and pretend that nothing had happened.

Janet was sitting at the far end of the bar. When she saw me, she hopped off the stool and disappeared.

Spencer stretched across the bar and took my hand, squeezing it a little too hard, pulled me close and whispered loudly in my ear, "Are you holding?"

"You're holding—my hand," I said.

"Were you in the bathroom just now?" he said.

"No," I said.

"Someone said they saw you."

"I look like a lot of people," I said.

"I haven't told the manager yet," said Spencer.

I didn't answer.

"I won't tell him," he said. "But you have to do me a favor."

"I SAID I'D DRIVE him home," was all I told Lucas before we left the bar.

"Don't," said Lucas. "I'll give him cab fare. Don't get in the car with him."

"He just wants a ride," I said.

"I don't trust him," said Lucas.

"He's too drunk to do anything," I said. I had no idea if that was true.

SPENCER DIRECTED ME, but I couldn't believe—didn't believe he lived in that neighborhood.

"Are we lost," I said. "This looks bad." I drove past tight row houses with boarded-up windows, and on the sidewalk, every block or so there'd be a young guy in a knit hat leaning against a burned out streetlight, watching us. I felt like the car was moving in slow motion. It was two-thirty in the morning.

"Pull over," said Spencer.

"I don't think that's a good idea," I said. I didn't know where I was. The street sign was missing; there was nothing but a pole. I was off the map.

"Pull over," he ordered me through clenched teeth.

I pulled up to the curb, engine running, at an hour when decent people are home in bed, and a man I'd never seen before, a black man too skinny for his clothing, leaned through the window that Spencer had opened and said, "Two rock for twenty." Spencer said something, and the guy jumped into the back seat of my car.

"Drive," said Spencer.

"No," I said.

"Are you fucking kidding me?" said Spencer. "Drive around the block. Now."

So I drove around the block.

"Pull over," he said. I did. The dealer got out. Spencer told me to drive again.

"Where?" I said. "I have no idea where we are."

"Just go forward," said Spencer. He pushed in my car's cigarette lighter. "Why is this taking so fucking long?" he said.

"It takes that long," I said. "How do I get to your house?" I knew he didn't live in that neighborhood.

He didn't answer right away. When the lighter was hot, he took it out and put one of his rocks on it and smoked it through an empty cardboard tube he must have kept in his jacket.

Spencer's crew cut was so blond you could see his pink scalp turning pinker the more he smoked. The stubble on his chin was so pale, it almost wasn't there. He was the whitest white boy I'd ever seen. I didn't know white boys like him smoked crack. I'd never seen any-one smoke crack before. Too many firsts for one night.

"Please tell me how to get to your house," I said. I was afraid I was going to cry. I didn't want Spencer to see that.

"Shut up," he said. "You're making too much noise. Shut up." His voice was full of menace.

I was silent, but the tears were going down my face. There wasn't anything I could do about that so I drove, with the smell of burning plastic, of vinyl seat-melt, of stripped inhibitions, of weak will.

Spencer tilted his head back and closed his eyes, breathed in and out too quickly, smoked some more. I followed his whispered di-rections to the good part of town, where the people were skinny on purpose. I let him out on a corner by a large brick Colonial. He walked off, jaunty like a sailor on shore leave, Gene Kelly in *On the Town*. As he approached the front steps where a lawn jockey painted white held up a ring, a motion sensor light blared on from above his head. I didn't wait for him to go inside.

I GOT HOME at four in the morning. I parked on the street across from the embassy. The Secret Service men nodded at me.

The light on my answering machine was blinking. I played the messages back. There were five, and they were all from Lucas, checking to see if I got home okay. The last one had been about twenty minutes ago. While I was listening to it, the phone rang. It was Lucas.

"I'm downstairs," he said.

"Oh no," I said.

"Let me in," he said, "before the goons arrest me."

I was glad the goons were guarding the empty headquarters of dispossessed Soviet diplomats and not the block where I'd just picked up a crack dealer.

I made Lucas tiptoe through the apartment to my bedroom.

"It's freezing in here," said Lucas. I handed him a sweatshirt. "That's not going to fit me," he said.

I told him about the nest. We went into the bathroom and looked out the window. It was done. There was a bird sitting on it.

"It's a dove," he said.

"That's so romantic," I said, and started to cry for real, with sound effects.

Without discussing it, we got into my bed and pulled the blanket over us. He put his arm around me, and we must have fallen asleep. When the sun came up, I awoke in the exact same position.

➔

I didn't get the job at the *Post*.

Before my contract was up, Madeline sent me for interviews at a few of her client's companies. When the aerospace company Jackson-Furlong asked me back a third time, they took me around to meet people. I was hired to be a liaison between the contract representatives who sold equipment to the military and the engineers who designed the equipment. I wasn't sure exactly what that would involve, but I liked the sound of "liaison." And I liked even more that the job would allow me to pay off my credit cards. Maybe I could even begin to save some money. I told my roommate I was moving.

One of the engineers I met that day was a man named Devin Shields. He was so tall he had to bend in doorways. He had a mustache and longish dirty-blond hair. He reminded me of William Hurt in *An Accidental Tourist*, cute, if on the pudgy side. He was introduced to me as the brains behind Furlong's innovative X-Series plane. I had no idea what that meant, but it sounded very 007 for a guy who was wearing a short-sleeved dress shirt. He had an air of always being preoccupied, and whenever I had reason to talk to him for work, he'd dash off as soon as the necessary conversation was done.

AT THE END of July, I met Lucas late one night, after he'd finished working at a wedding reception.

I said, "Let's not to go to Heaven."

"Agreed," he said.

Instead we went to Childe Harold, at Dupont Circle.

I told Lucas I was moving. "The birds are gone," I said, "and I'm going, too." The nest had been empty for weeks. Whoever took my place would be able to shut the window if they wanted.

"You could take the nest with you," he said. "For luck."

"Is it lucky?" I said.

"Doves," he said.

Lucas had some news, too. "I'm going," he said. "In September. It's cheaper then, and there are fewer tourists."

"I'm happy for you," I said.

"I wish you could come," he said.

We toasted his trip and my new job, and then he said, "Who is he?"

"Who?" I said.

"Come on," he said. "There's always someone, and you haven't mentioned anyone in weeks."

"There might be someone," I said. "I'm not sure."

"Whatever you say," said Lucas.

IN LATE SEPTEMBER, I received a postcard with a photo on the front showing a jumble of red tile rooftops. Splashed across the bottom of the photo in big green letters were the words "Dubrovnik 1989."

"You'd love it here," said the message on the back. *"Meeting fabulous people; staying longer, traveling around. Will let you know where I end up. Blowing kisses across the sea! L."*

I tacked the postcard to the padded wall of my cubicle and imagined Lucas wandering on cobbled streets hidden below those rooftops.

ABOUT A MONTH later, I received a postcard from Oslo:

"Too $$$ here, but the people are beautiful. Took a job in the kitchen of an inn at the edge of the world—going tomorrow. More soon! XOX Lucas"

That was the last time I heard from him.

➜

A few days after I received the first postcard, Devin stopped by my cubicle. His project had fallen behind schedule. The plane wasn't quite working yet, but I was beginning to learn that there was nothing unusual about that. This time he didn't run off immediately after giving me the standard paperwork, which I was supposed to organize and type and pass along to my boss.

Devin pointed to the postcard of Dubrovnik on my wall and said, "Have you been?"

"No," I said. I started to say I was supposed to go, and I couldn't afford it, but I only said, "I'd like to, though. A friend sent me that."

"It's a fascinating place," said Devin. "A beautiful place. Pre-Christian, settled by Greek sailors." It was the first thing he'd said to me that had nothing to do with work. In his voice was a hint of almost childlike excitement, as if he was eager for me to know about it—not as if he wanted to teach me, but as if he wanted me to understand so that I could feel excited about it the way he did—the real Dubrovnik.

"I didn't know that," I said.

He stood there, hands in his trouser pockets, rocking back and forth on his heels, and then nodded at the papers. "Let me know if there are any questions about that," he said, and walked off.

The next day, he was back at my cubicle. "Am I interrupting?" he said. There was a mechanical pencil tucked behind his ear, and his hair was combed more neatly than usual.

"No," I said. I was typing up notes from that morning's meeting. My typing speed hadn't improved, but no one at Furlong seemed to care about that.

"Would you like to have lunch in the cafeteria with me?" said Devin.

I could see his undershirt peeking from between the buttons of his dress shirt, the mole below his collarbone, and the blush that was creeping up his neck as he stood there over my desk, like a white candle, lit.

I said yes.

TRANSFIGURED NIGHT

My new boss, Chick, was a morbidly obese manic off his meds who hailed from a tiny town I'd never heard of—Wassily, Louisiana—a town so small, Chick claimed, the shotgun shacks only had space for pistols. In summers, he told me, you wished for a pistol to shoot your wife or maybe end it all, what with the stillborn air, the chiggers, the mold. I told him my family had lived without air-conditioning in D.C. until I was nine, so I knew something about swampy heat. He didn't respond—he practically ignored me—and I didn't mention the tiny brick house, which was still superior to anything that might be called a shack.

Chick was a private consultant, but what anyone might be consulting him about was a mystery. I kept his calendar, I wrote his correspondence, I made charts, and I brought him foot-long Italian subs for lunch, dripping with oil and vinegar and shedding lettuce, which he consumed in three large bites. He was a neat eater, though. When he was done, no evidence remained because he always disposed of his food trash in my office garbage can instead of his. He'd walk into my office on some pretense, holding the crumpled oily brown paper and the Styrofoam clamshell, slyly drop it in the trash, and leave. I'd smell mortadella for the rest of the day.

WORKING FOR CHICK was a serious demotion from the work I'd been doing at Furlong, but I'd had to find something else quickly. It was for a good reason: I was getting married.

Before we were engaged, Devin had designed an airplane that flew sorties in Desert Storm. There was a scale model on the coffee table in what used to be Devin's but what was now our apartment. I'd teased him about the plane being a design feature in the apartment, and suggested we hang an open parachute from the ceiling. Devin wasn't amused. I was proud of him about the plane, even though I hadn't agreed with the war, which everyone seemed to know was only about Kuwait's oil, but at Furlong we pretended that it wasn't, that it had been a noble cause.

Our boss at Furlong gave us symphony tickets for a wedding gift, a season of concerts to go with our newlywed year. He also gave us a letter that said one of us had to leave. The company didn't allow employees to be married; it was a security risk. I laughed when I read that part—"security risk." Because wasn't it a security risk to draw diagrams of military planes while in the audience at a concert hall? Devin never knew when he'd get an idea for a project he was working on. Even at the symphony, he'd scribble these diagrams in the program, then tear out the pages and stick them in his suit jacket. I'd find the pages when I took the suit to the cleaners. He'd come home from work and say, "Have you seen . . ." And I'd say, "Sorry, I sold them to the Russians," and then I'd hand him the papers.

I was the one who left Furlong, because I was only an assistant. I wasn't broken up about leaving, but it was unfair. Devin might have at least offered to be the one to go. Even if he didn't mean it, and we both knew it would be the wrong decision. The thing about Devin, he was always just exactly who he was. To suggest something he didn't mean to follow through on wouldn't even occur to him. He wouldn't have understood the point. This was one of the qualities I liked about him when we first started dating. I still did. Most of the time.

"Maybe we shouldn't get married," I'd said to Devin, when we got that letter. I was half afraid he'd take me seriously, but that didn't stop me from making the joke. I wanted to get married. And I'd decided that Devin must be The One, or pretty damn close, because he didn't pin me by the wrists to keep me still when we were having sex, nor did he have a job that would ever be described using the word "gig." He wasn't a thrill ride—he was reliable, he was true, he had a quiet strength. Marrying was supposed to be about settling down, which I imagined as even-tempered contentment; in marriage, I was convinced, "exciting" really spelled "disaster." And I thought Devin would make a good father, if that situation came up, since as I well knew, it could come up despite my intentions to the contrary. He would be a good example for a child—a better example than I'd proved to be so far.

I was as sure about Devin as I could have been. He, on the other hand, had not consistently demonstrated a certainty equal to mine. He'd given me few clues, veiled references to a shared future. "Someday we'll go to Dubrovnik, when it's safe," he'd promised. "Someday I'll teach you to drive a stick." Until one day, down on one knee and the whole thing. What took him so long? I didn't ask. When someone asks you to marry him, "What took you so long, buster?" isn't a welcome reply. Later, I got around to asking myself if that silent waiting had been a mistake on my part. Because if that was our first big decision together, shouldn't we have talked about it in more concrete terms?

A year and a month later, the idea of a husband was still strange to me. It was hard to say it—"husband"—without feeling like I was acting, or like I was one of those gushy women who waves her ring finger around to her single friends when it's already old news. Did little girls still play house? "You pour the tea, while I rock the baby to sleep." I'd never played those games. I felt like I was playing them now.

➜

A week ago, Chick handed me a hundred dollars in cash, bonus pay for a project that went overtime. And then, a day ago, he called me a "huge fucking disappointment," because of a typo in one of the letters I wrote for him. My degree was in cultural anthropology, knowledge I had yet to apply in any formal way unless you counted trenchant observations about bosses in their sociocultural context. I didn't remember Clifford Geertz mentioning the significance of typing skills in his essay about cockfighting.

That afternoon, I walked to the sub shop in a daze, Chick's epithet still ringing in my skull. The sullen teenage boy behind the counter, playing drums with the breadsticks, snickered and jabbed his hot sister with his elbow when she handed me the order.

"What's so funny?" I asked.

"My brother thinks you're skinny for eating one of those every day," she said.

"It's not for me," I said. "It's for Chick."

They looked at each other. "Chick told us you'd say that," said the boy.

"You believed him?" I said.

"Too skinny even though you barf it up," the boy said, and stuck his finger in his gaping mouth and made authentic gagging sounds while his eyes bulged as if he might really vomit any second.

"Chick said I do that?" I said. That asshole. I didn't make myself vomit. That was over long before Chick knew me.

"Glarg," the boy gagged harder.

"Marco," said his sister, smacking him on the arm. "Sorry for him," she told me. Then she leaned over the counter and said, "He's a little slow." She tapped her temple with a bright pink fingernail. "He says things, he doesn't know any better," she said. "He doesn't mean it."

I watched him lurch away, the lumpy gait, the odd slant of his shoulders and tilt of his head—I was surprised I hadn't noticed before.

"It's okay," I said. "I have a sister like that."

Her eyes popped a little. "You do?" she said. "We should introduce them."

"Oh that's nice," I said. "But my sister's a little old for him." He looked to be around seventeen. My sister was already Devin's age, thirty-three.

She looked terribly disappointed to hear that. Another person I'd disappointed in the space of a couple of hours. I bought a jar of Nutella because I felt bad about the whole thing, and then I thanked them and left.

When I'd announced that Devin and I were getting married, my sister had said, "The eldest daughter is supposed to get married first." Her vision of the world was black and white and based primarily on what she read, which she accepted as fact no matter where she read it, from *USA Today* to Lyndon LaRouche campaign brochures.

My mother, on the other hand, was perfectly mentally able, or so I'd been led to believe. She'd puffed on her cigarette and said in an approving stage whisper, "He wears socks."

➔

"Why do we have Nutella?" said Devin, his head in the refrigerator.

We were supposed to be leaving for the symphony soon, but he was still in his undershirt. When he put on a dress shirt, I could see the V-neck of the undershirt beneath it. Devin's lack of interest in preening was another one of those qualities I initially found endearing. It was becoming difficult to separate the approvals from the disapprovals and small matters from big ones, all of it getting heaped into a big basket of frustration. It occurred to me that because I was hating my job, a lot of other things were going to frustrate me.

"I have to leave my job," I said.

"Again?" said Devin.

"My boss is a nutcase," I said.

"That's not an attractive word," he said. He could be so prim. When we met, I'd had enough of the fast-talking charming types who couldn't sit still long enough for a relationship. I liked that Devin was serious. Except—

"I'm sorry," I said. "My boss is a bilious troglodyte. His monogrammed cuffs are stained with mustard, and he's a bad tipper. He calls welfare mothers 'lazy leeches on society,' and he stares at my chest. Better?"

Devin stared at my face. "Calm down," he said. "It doesn't help to get worked up about it."

"See, that's where we differ," I said. "I think getting worked up is perfectly normal, even required, in this situation. It's not normal to always be so controlled. When I was a kid, my friend's mom died of an aneurysm. From holding it all in. All of a sudden pfffft," I said. "She was forty."

"I'm not normal?" he said.

"*It's*," I said.

"This is an opportunity to examine our goals," Devin said in his lecturing voice.

"Okay," I said. *Our* goals?

"I don't think you should keep working for someone who treats you that way," he said. "I agree with that."

"Thank you," I said.

"We've talked about other choices, too," he said.

He meant children. How could he talk to me about having children and at the same time make me feel like a child?

"I want to go back to school. I need at least a master's, maybe a PhD, to be employable."

Devin had a master's in engineering.

"A PhD in what?" he said. "What about kids?"

"I don't think I can get a graduate degree in childbearing."

He wanted me to go off the Pill. It was the same argument we'd had before. Though we'd had only a year of marriage to pick our fights, I couldn't help believing that we'd already settled into them in a way that would last. I'd told him I didn't want children. I'd told him why—my sister. I'd told him that I'd seen the deceptive snowballs that life could aim at you, the ones packed with a big rock in the center. My sister was once a beautiful chubby baby—I'd seen the photographs. Nothing about her at that time indicated the problems that lay ahead.

"I don't want to be one of those old dads who can't keep up on the playground," he said.

"You're hardly old," I said. "But you might want to let your hair down a little, emotively speaking, so you don't get an aneurysm on the playground."

He refused to be goaded. "It's not going to happen again," he said, meaning I wasn't going to have a child like my sister. As if he could predict that.

A child like my sister. My parents were counting on me to supervise my sister's life when they were no longer able. Sometimes I wondered if they'd decided to have a second child in order to make sure their fragile firstborn would always have a keeper. When I married Devin, their relief had been palpable, as if marriage had suddenly turned me into someone selfless and reliable.

"You can be stubborn, Miranda," said Devin.

"Thanks, but I don't need your permission."

He puffed out his cheeks and released the air in a chuff of exasperation. How could I have once found that tic endearing?

He walked away. "I'm getting dressed," he called from the bedroom.

THE SPECTER OF my sister wasn't the whole story behind my resistance to having children. I didn't tell him that I'd had the chance for a child once, a chance I'd rejected for the best and worst reasons, and I didn't know if I'd ever want another.

WE GOT TO the concert just in time, Devin driving too fast, his one dangerous habit. I didn't mind; in fact, it was a turn-on, the feel of the speeding car, the lack of control, watching Devin let go for once. We took our seats in the Red Room, what I called the concert hall—red velvet, red flat carpet, red satin ceiling, like being inside a giant heart. We were formal and overly solicitous with each other, both of us afraid to cause further offense. I put my hand on his wrist.

The music began, and Devin held my hand. With his other hand, he took up the binoculars to look at the cellist, and my warm feelings dissipated. I didn't know her name; I called her Brenda Starr because of her long red hair. Devin didn't know that I knew he watched her. What were binoculars if not a device to permit intimate study without actual intimacy? He could watch without the cellist knowing, and he could think he'd fooled me, too, our intimacy somehow also distant even though no physical lens was in our way.

Devin's mouth opened and his grip on my hand relaxed. His Adam's apple rose and fell, as if he took direction in his swallowing from the conductor. Devin's slight hunch, his receded chin and prominent forehead, his thinning blond hair a little too long and looped behind his ear reminded me of a giant bird stalking its lovely prey—because the cellist *was* lovely, her lush auburn hair, worn loose, brushed the sides of her instrument when she played, and her stark white décolletage was framed by her hair and the cello. But I exaggerate, because Devin was handsome in his own way, only not as much when I was angry.

The orchestra played, and I searched the President's box for Hillary Clinton, and Devin drew pictures in the program. I scanned the musicians to see if my favorites were there. I had my own crush on a double-bass player I'd named Apollo, because he looked like a Greek god, someone Michelangelo might have seen fit to paint—aquiline nose, black eyes and close-cropped black hair. Through our binoculars, I watched as he rubbed rosin along the bow with his pale, delicate fingers. I imagined those fingers around the reins of a chariot pulling the rising sun across the sky.

How odd that I could see him clearly through those lenses. I could make out the fine contours of his ear in as much detail as I could see Devin's, right beside me. Our seats were orchestra-left, and I had to lean at an obnoxious angle vis-a-vis the woman next to me in order to see Apollo, so I satisfied myself with occasional glimpses, which made him all the more attractive. As a consolation, I absorbed myself in the frenetic movements of the conductor, a man who looked like a broken-nosed character actor playing the thug on *Law & Order*. And yet he had a gorgeous, talented wife, an opera singer, and he was a notorious womanizer; the soloists he invited were always beautiful women. I decided he must have a regular lover in the orchestra, and the way she gazed at him, a piteous and solemn gaze worthy of a pilgrim at a religious shrine, I could only believe his lover was Brenda Starr.

I read the program notes on the piece that had just begun—Schoenberg's *Verklärte Nacht, Transfigured Night*. I'd never heard it

97

before. It struck me first as melodramatic, the musical equivalent of a Daphne du Maurier novel, ethereal violin arrested by the dark portent of bass. I might have been right. Here's where it got sticky: the program told me Schoenberg had been inspired by a poem in which a man and woman take a walk at night in the woods. The woman is distraught and tells the man she's carrying a child that isn't his, a pregnancy from an old lover before the two had met. The man calms her worries and assures her that he'll raise this other man's baby as his own.

The man and the woman lived happily ever after, or so we were meant to believe. A fairy tale. Which explained the way the music seemed to demand, and receive, its particular emotional response: Now be afraid, now relieved, now content, now love.

In real life there were no happy endings to stories that start with a woman saying, "It's not yours." But something in the way the story was told inside that music made me a victim of its emotional manipulation, until I no longer felt manipulated.

Brenda Starr was in first chair for the Schoenberg. She hugged her cello, pressed its body to her body, her right breast crushed against it. The conductor wagged his fingers at her, waved her off without a glance. He pulled taffy, he scolded like a schoolmarm, and still she beamed up at him. He grasped the blank air above her head and dragged it to his chest. The musicians, all of them, instantly obeyed, swaying and purring as one animal, while he stroked them under his palm. At the end, when he pointed to direct applause to the stand-out performers, she wasn't among them.

➺

Devin and I didn't talk much during intermission, just drank the gin and tonics we'd ordered beforehand and stared at the sea of people in seemingly identical suits and black dresses, listened to the low-grade hum of their talk instead. I was thinking about the Schoenberg. Maybe Devin was hearing music in his head, too. I held my drink with one hand and with the other held onto Devin's elbow, and he bent and kissed me and we went back to drinking.

I once persuaded him to have sex with me in the laundry room at his parents' house, before we were engaged. There was the blam blam blam of our bodies banging against the Sears Roebuck washing machine, the smell of damp towels, of something else, like old apple cores. He'd lifted me up and I could see down his back, the mole on his shoulder blade, his naked ass, his pants gathered at his feet. His parents hadn't heard us. Their room was on the far side of the house, near the two separate ones where we were supposed to be sleeping. Sometimes I thought that was when he'd decided to marry me.

➔

On the way home from the concert, we were subdued, as if the mood of our earlier argument had been diluted but not entirely eliminated by the music. I was trying to play back the Schoenberg in my head. It had lulled me in a way I wasn't used to. But in my mind it was off, misremembered, flat, sharp, lacking crescendos, as if an inept student practiced it in my brain. We drove through the park, the scenic route, though there was nothing to see in the dark. No street lights, winding road, and only one lane in each direction, woods on either side, rushing by in a blur of star-punctured night.

Then it stopped. Something massive flew at our faces, blotted out the road, piercing squeal and screech and there was a snap and skid and bump and we were up on the grass just short of a tree, our headlights cutting into the woods and all was quiet. We sat there for what seemed like a long time, just breathing; I could hear Devin breathing. I wasn't conscious of any other sound. We were pinned by the airbags. I moved my fingers to make sure I could, wiggled my toes inside my tight shoes.

"What the hell?" said Devin, finally.

"You folks all right?" said a man outside, a voice I didn't recognize. A white light shone through the open car window. I had to look twice to know it wasn't the moon. Neither of us answered right away.

Then Devin said, "I think so, yes." And he touched my arm, "Miranda?"

"I'm okay," although I wasn't sure. I'd had the wind knocked out of me.

"I called it in on my CB," said the man.

A tree branch had punched the front windshield and was jutting into the car, dead center.

No, not a tree branch.

A hoof.

"Oh no," I said. I leaned on the door, as if to get out. The car felt too close to the ground.

"Stay put," said the man outside. "Wait for an EMT."

I couldn't see him very well because the road was unlit, and his light half-blinded me, and the glare of our own headlights made an obscuring aura, throwing into silhouette the thing that I was beginning to make out on the hood of our car.

"Y'all are lucky," the man said. He pointed his light at the hood then back at us. "She's a big one." And then it became dark again, and I realized he was walking away, and the one sound I could hear was the rumbling of his engine. I'd assumed he was a policeman, but in the rearview mirror, which was, incredibly, still intact, I watched him walk to his pick-up, several yards behind us in the grass.

There was no shoulder, and I could see now that our car was partly blocking the road. A few cars went around us.

The man came back. "Guess you got insurance," I heard him say, *tsk*ing over the condition of our car.

Devin got out. "Stay here," he said to me. I saw him look at the hood and put his hand over his mouth and walk away. That's when I realized that what I'd thought was rain spattering the cracked windshield was actually blood.

I wasn't going to sit there alone. If he could get out so could I. I could handle it. Devin didn't know what I'd handled already.

When I got out of the car, my heel sank into the grass. It had rained during the concert. My feet were instantly damp. My body felt sore, like I'd slept for too long in the wrong position. I saw that the tire on my side was flat, the wheel well and the area above were crushed like a can someone had stepped on. The deer was splayed on its side on the hood at a diagonal. It must have slid on its haunch when it landed. Its hind leg was the one that broke the windshield. Its belly rose and fell with agitated breathing. Its head rested above the grill, and I could see the white of its eye and the huge black pupil and the muzzle bright with blood. While I watched, its tongue flicked out to try and lick the blood away. There was a sigh that became a groan, and I felt Devin's hand on my back, his arm going around me, turning me away. I'd made the sound.

"I told you to stay in the car," he said, his arm locked around me, trapping my bent arm to my side. I bit my finger.

Devin led me to the grassy area between our car and the pick-up.

"Thank you," I said to the stranger. "Thank you for stopping."

The man cleared his throat every minute or so, like a heavy smoker. His hair was long and stringy and the color of rust. He had a wide face and several days' beard growth. I was conscious of our clothes, my long tight skirt and silk blouse, me and Devin dressed for our fancy night out, the stranger in an Army surplus jacket. Devin was tall enough to be intimidating. Just in case. He sometimes had to bend in doorways.

"You don't have to wait," Devin told him.

The man had bushy eyebrows and now he raised them, like humped caterpillars. "Coulda been us, hit that deer," he said.

"Parish?" The door of the pick-up banged shut, and we all spun and looked. A woman was getting out of the passenger side. "You said you'd tell me if they were okay," she said, coming toward us. There was a hole in the knee of her jeans and her sweater was too tight around her thick waist. Her hair was short and sticking out in places.

"Are you okay?" she said to me. She had eyes the color of slate, with dark crescents of liner smeared underneath.

I nodded.

"Don't do that," said Parish. But the woman either hadn't heard or didn't listen, because she walked past me to the front of our car.

"Poor Bambi," she said. "Look, she's still breathing."

I didn't want to tell her that it was Bambi's mother that gets killed. And that was by a hunter. And Bambi was a male. Like my degree, what I did know about things rarely seemed useful.

"Vick," said Parish. "Don't. Come on now." And he pulled her away by the arm.

"Shouldn't we shoot her?" said Vick. "She's suffering."

"Police are coming," said Parish.

"Maybe the police'll shoot it?" said Vick.

"Doubt it," said Parish. "They don't like the paperwork."

"It's not right," said Vick.

I walked away, around their truck. There was a storage bin set into the bed of the pick-up, with a big padlock on it. There were only two options for what was stored in that type of box, only two categories of items people were worried about locking up: tools, if you were a contractor; guns, if you were a hunter.

"We were coming up the other side there, and I saw her in the road," Vick was saying when I came back. "Doe was just standing there. She saw our lights, froze, Parish slammed the brakes."

"She sprung away like a giant rabbit," said Parish. "Jumped right in front of your car, hardly hit the ground before she was on your hood."

"That's what it felt like," said Devin. "Out of nowhere."

"Parish pulled around to see if y'all were okay," said Vick. "Coulda been us," she said, as if no one had said it yet. She curled her arm through Parish's arm and rubbed her belly. "He hit the brakes so hard, I hit the dash. I think I bruised my ribs."

"Told you to wear your seatbelt," said Parish.

"I hate being held in," she said to me, as if I was the one who needed to understand. "Don't like tight places."

"I've seen where the airbags don't open," said Parish. "Y'all are lucky in all ways but one tonight." His glance flicked me up and down.

"You far from home?" Vick said.

"Only fifteen minutes," I said.

Devin gave me an exasperated look that meant, Don't tell them where we live.

"We live in Takoma," said Vick. "Parish used to live in George-town. We were on our way to see friends."

Georgetown was the realm of buttoned-up preppies. "Why Georgetown?" I said. I couldn't help myself. Devin gave me another look.

"I was in school," said Parish. "Mechanical engineering."

Devin perked up. "Really?" he said. "You're in that field?" Don't sound so surprised, I wanted to tell him.

"Was," said Parish. "I went overseas for a while."

I imagined Parish dropping out of his engineering program, even though he'd excelled at it, even though he could build or fix just about anything. I imagined he thought the microchip was for people who didn't know how things really worked.

"Huh," said Devin. It was almost sad how deflated he looked.

"The Army," said Vick. "They paid his way. He was in Kuwait."

"Desert Storm?" I said, like Kuwait could have meant anything else.

"Yeah," said Parish. "Flew helicopters. And maintenance, helicopter maintenance."

"Devin designed a plane they used there," I said.

Devin had his arm around my waist, and when I said that he squeezed me hard like he wanted to cut off my breathing.

"You did," said Parish. It didn't sound like a question. "The F-23?"

"Yes, that one," I said, but Devin was saying, "No."

"I guess I had it wrong," I said. But the plaque on the model in our apartment said "Operation Desert Storm, F-23." Devin's department had given it to him in '91, shortly before we were engaged and after the air war ended.

"Mine was a prototype," said Devin. "Never flew."

THE POLICE CAR pulled up with its flashing red light. A tow-truck showed up a few minutes later. The policeman shined his flashlight over our car for a perfunctory second, and then the men conferred.

Vick and I walked around the car and stood in the headlights. Three giant birds, black and gaunt with red bald spots and large hooked beaks had landed in the grass nearby.

"Turkey vultures," said Vick. "A doe that size has a lot of meals in it."

"Won't they at least wait until it's dead?" I said.

"Sure," she said. "But it's too good to waste on them."

"You mean, you'd eat that deer?"

"Why not?"

"I didn't know you could eat the deer that lived around here," I said, knowing how it sounded even as I said it.

"You think there are special ones they make just for cooking?" said Vick and laughed until she was bent over.

"I guess that was pretty stupid."

"It's all right, honey," said Vick. "I needed a laugh."

"There are too many deer," said Parish, returning. "But you don't like them to suffer."

"Isn't he sensitive?" said Vick, still laughing.

"What's so funny?" he asked.

"We took over their land with two-car garages," I said. "And then we're surprised when they walk in front of a car."

"That's not funny," said Parish.

"Never mind," I said. I wandered off, making divots in the grass with my spikey heels.

"What's with her?" I heard Parish say behind me.

I thought of my sister, the other suffering deer. Just by being alive, she threatened the life I wanted for myself. I resented her, and I didn't think much of myself for that.

I went up to Devin, where he was talking with the tow-truck driver.

"Go sit in the back of the police car," said Devin. "He'll take us home as soon as this guy can move the car. Looks like we're going to need a new one. What kind do you want? Maserati? Lotus?"

"Who cares," I said.

"You hate that car," said Devin. "I thought you'd be glad to get a new one."

He was right. I never liked the car. It was an old Taurus.

"If it wasn't such a tank," said Devin, "things might be much worse right now."

"Right," I said. "I'm glad the deer killed our crappy car."

"Now you're being ridiculous," he said. "Again."

"You had to get that in, didn't you?"

"We're not doing this here," he said.

I glanced around and saw that Parish and Vick were pointedly not looking in our direction.

"Where should we do it then?" I said.

"Shush," said Devin.

"Shush?" I said. "Like I'm an infant?"

"I don't know," said Devin. "I only know you don't want one." He started to turn away and then turned back to me and said, "Only selfish people don't want children."

Right away, he looked stunned that he'd said it. I backed away, and my heel got stuck. I slid my foot out of my shoe and left the shoe there, hobbled to the police car and got into the back seat.

"Please take me home," I said. "My husband wants to stay with the car. The truck driver will bring him home."

The policeman peered over his seat at me. "You okay, ma'am?" he said.

"Yes," I said.

I saw through the windshield that Devin was looking at the police car, but I knew the headlights' glare would keep him from seeing me.

"Ma'am, why don't you look down at the seat now and cover your ears."

"Why?" I said.

"I recommend it," said the policeman.

And then over his radio's static I heard the shot and an echo of the shot.

The policeman had let Parish shoot the deer. He sat in his car and pretended not to notice.

"He shot it?" I said dumbly.

"I don't know," said the policeman. "If I knew someone fired a weapon, I'd have to report it. So I hope not."

I opened the door and stepped out to look. The pick-up had been moved so that its bed faced our hood. The tow truck's winch was already lifting the dead deer off our car. Everything seemed murky and distant and unintelligible, obscured as it was by darkness, by the sounds of engines idling, a faraway siren, the cop's radio banter. I wished for the binoculars; I needed to be closer without being closer. I needed to see. But I'd forgotten them in the car. They were too large for my purse and I'd put them on the floor, by my feet, for the drive home. I'd seen Devin empty the glove box, but in the confusion, he probably hadn't remembered to look for the binoculars. I would have remembered because they'd once belonged to my grandfather, who'd used them—so my mother said—to watch birds. What I knew about my grandfather told me that "birds" was a euphemism.

I heard the policeman say, "I wouldn't." But I walked to the car, to the passenger door, which was still open the way I'd left it. No one else saw me. They were all watching the process of moving the deer. Its legs dangled in the air. There was a tarp wrapped around its middle. I bent to search the floor of the car. It was too dark down there to see much. I felt around the chunks of glass and found the binoculars jammed under the seat. I took them out of the case and put the strap around my neck and went behind the car. I looked through them, adjusting the lenses for the new distance. The deer's neck drooped. Its mouth hung open and its eyes were black and dull. Its teeth were bared and a crust of blood lined its mouth like ghastly lipstick.

I went back to the police car, got inside and shut the door. The cop handed me a box of tissues. Then he pulled onto the road.

➔

I was asleep in my clothes on the bed when Devin got home. I'd cut my hands on the glass searching for the binoculars and now my fingers were wrapped in Band-Aids. Devin tiptoed into our room and slipped under the covers. I opened my eyes and stared at the ceiling.

"Are you awake?" he asked.

"Yes," I said.

"I'm sorry," he said, taking my hand and kissing one of the Band-Aids.

"Me, too," I said, snuggling up to him.

"You shouldn't have said that about the airplane," he said.

"What?"

"About my airplane."

It took me a minute to remember. "I was making conversation," I said. "He was over there."

"Exactly why you don't tell him," said Devin. "You don't know what he experienced."

"I didn't know you felt guilty about it," I said.

"What?" he said. He let go of my hand and sat up in bed in the dark.

"I didn't know you felt bad that they used it," I said. "If you design something that blows things up, don't you think things might get blown up?"

"You need to be more discreet," he said.

"I thought this was the make-up part," I said. I put my hand on his knee. I still desperately wanted this—whatever it was that was happening—to stop.

"I thought it was, too." Devin gathered up the blanket that was folded at the foot of the bed and left the room.

➔

The moment before the impact, when I was trying to locate the music in my head, what I wanted to recapture was the wholeness I felt all too briefly when I'd first heard it. When I listened, as I read the story told by the poem, something had happened to me, as if I'd taken the music like a pill, swallowed it. It filled my insides, a feeling that was familiar, even though I'd never heard that music before. The threatening bass, those lighthearted violins, that drama, rising and resolving—It was resolution I wanted, the kind that was only possible in stories.

JUMP

I STAND ON the balcony and look over the rail. I consider the possible trajectory that would result in a crushed vial of lip gloss, a pocket of exploded sugarplum, but a cell phone that is still perfect and spared, where the voice that will live forever is stored, where you can shout your message into the wind, even when it's clear that its owner can never be reached.

Behind me, my parents—no, still our parents—insist on the possibility of an intruder, and the prescribing psychiatrist sits on my sister's couch—though she's no longer his patient, so perhaps it's not a breach.

I can see the wet concrete, where the staff hosed off the deck and pool water splashed over the edge and people walked through it, leaving dark footprints. The sign by the pool says "No lifeguard on duty. Swim at your own risk." I can see the brown skin of a girl in a string bikini, her navel ring glinting in the sun like a homing device. When she's hot enough, she jumps into the pool, treads water, climbs back out, and sits a few minutes to dry off. Then she pulls on spandex shorts, slaps flip-flops across the deck, and rides up in the elevator to her boyfriend who was asleep in the apartment before, but who is now pacing, talking on the phone and making toast. When she comes in, no one catches the door, it slams behind her, the flip-flops come off. The girl and her boyfriend embrace, he gets down on his knees and nuzzles her belly, flicking the ring with his tongue. He slips off the bottom half of her bikini, and the two of them land together on the floor with a thud. The toast pops up but no one does anything about it.

I HEAR ALL of this as I pace on parquet flooring that's identical to theirs. At first I thoughtlessly mimic the boyfriend's path back and forth—What will I learn by pacing it out? How many steps to the door? How many to the toaster? How many to the sofa? The sliding glass door? The toilet? I count the steps, but it tells me nothing, and meanwhile my/our parents speculate and the psychiatrist bemoans, dejected, combing fingers through sparse hair in a way that calms him, like raking sand in a Zen garden. I consider where the couple upstairs might have been a few hours ago, when the pool was not yet open, and when my sister looked down at the wet concrete and saw a solution.

I NAME THE girl Angela and her boyfriend Jimmy, but not the Jimmy I had a crush on in high school, he would be older by now. Angela works in retail, but this is her day off. She bought the bikini as soon as it went on sale, with her employee discount. Jimmy works in a bank. He looks younger than he is. I want to ask them what they heard four hours ago, or were they making love in the bedroom then and not on the beige carpet in the middle of the living room where he caught his heel on the edge of the coffee table and cried out? Was the bedroom door closed? Were the windows closed? The vertical blinds that led to the balcony? If they had not been in their bedroom fucking, if the girl, if Angela had not been moaning (as she is now, moaning like a porn star, like she thinks she should sound—I am critical of her moaning, I have just lost my sister, I have no patience for Angela's fraudulent performance), if she had been quiet, would she have heard, over Jimmy's grunting, which is not fake and cannot be mistaken for grunting of any other sort, would she have heard the clatter of vertical blinds that my sister merely pushed aside but didn't bother opening with the cord, or the metallic screech of the door to the balcony sliding open? Would they have heard the clunk of the plant being knocked over as my sister swung her leg over the railing? The plant, which won't die, although its loose topsoil is scattered in a distinct pattern over the tiles—a pattern that warrants further analysis—and whose pot is cracked up one side, though we cannot be sure this crack was not there before. But we want to understand; it can't be helped. We all have our different explanations. Me, my/our parents, the psychiatrist, the first person to arrive at the pool this morning, who found an unpleasant surprise on the deck and called 911, who will never get my sister's face out of his mind, who will in fact go to therapy to try, and it will mostly work, he will not always see her broken body in his imagination while he is sitting on a deck chair, or when he is swimming laps and comes up for air, but he will, on the rare occasion when he gets up the nerve to walk out to the end of the diving board and stand there on the sandpapery surface with his toes curled over the edge. Then he will see her hand, even though he will move across town and then finally to another state because of his job, he will still see her hand and the way it was turned out, and the small scrapes on the pads of her fingers.

ANGELA AND JIMMY, who don't even know their downstairs neighbor, the one who might have, once or twice, played her music too loudly too late at night; who might have cried on the telephone once too often; who definitely set her alarm clock to wake to the news station and forgot to turn it off so that weather and traffic were reported every seven minutes into eternity, but who was, otherwise, a good enough neighbor to have in a high-rise apartment building—Angela and Jimmy would regret my sister's absence because she would soon be replaced by a woman with a small child whose whereabouts and activities would always be too obvious to them to pretend they didn't notice. Because the truth was, the truth *was* that Jimmy heard a "funny noise" when he got up to get a rubber this morning. He was annoyed about the rubber, but Angela forgot her pill, and she insisted. His rubbers were really old, he told her that. It could be they had expired. He rummaged through a cigar box containing postage stamps with not enough value now that the cost had increased and loose Tic Tacs and that matchbook from Mexico and a picture of his old girlfriend, topless with her finger in her mouth, and it was true that he loved Angela, but—rubbers. And as he stood locating the packet, about to tear it open right there in the kitchen and massage it onto his penis, he heard a sound, like a dull knock, and a wheezing, like the air leaving a balloon, and a thunk. Was it a thunk? He froze and then turned his head toward the sound. He remembered taking several of these same rubbers, filling them with water, and dropping them over the balcony, one drunken night. He remembered the sound they made hitting the pavement, while Angela who was down there and drunk herself, coming home late with her girlfriends, had shouted at him from below. He remembered what he was supposed to be doing with the rubber this time, looked down at his cock, gave it a couple quick strokes, and slipped on the overcoat.

➜

Jumping is an impulse based on an opportunity. When they put barriers along the sides of the Duke Ellington Bridge, people stopped jumping. There's another bridge a few blocks away, but they don't go to that bridge, they just don't jump. Maybe they go home and slash their wrists. But I don't think the people who are jumping and the people who are cutting their wrists open are in the same demographic group. If you slash your wrists, you're going to have to deal with blood before you pass out, but if you jump, it's someone else's problem. Now, the way my sister did it, the outcome might have been different. She might have been paralyzed. She didn't think it through. This was her hallmark; she did not think things through. She needed me for that. But she never asked me. There's a news story about a local man who jumped off the roof of his house and landed on the driveway. He didn't fall very far, but he fell just the right way, and he died. The newspaper containing this story is folded up in a magazine rack next to the toilet in Donna's bathroom. Did she read it? Did she think about this man and what led him to carry the ladder from the garage and lean it up against the back of the house when no one was home? To sit on his roof killing a six-pack and tossing the empties into his wife's flower garden? Did Donna tire of listening to Jimmy and Angela go at it day after day while she had no boyfriend, while she heard no grunting that originated on her side of the drywall? But that is mundane. If I could imagine what led her to launch herself over the railing, I might do it, too. I swing one leg up, hooking my foot over the railing. In my imagination, I'm graceful, more than I ever was in the three months of ballet classes where another girl, one who was clumsy but fast and strong enough to tackle me, pinched my legs through the pink tights and left bruises.

➜

If I keep looking at this plant in the broken pot and don't look past it, I will not figure out what happened to my sister. I'm going to have to walk back inside the apartment and look at my mother, who got dressed in a hurry this morning, who is smoking despite her heart, but she just lost her daughter, her other daughter, so I'll allow it. I will look at my father, who is holding her shoulders and ignoring the smoke for the first time in years.

THEY DON'T SAY anything when I walk out to the balcony. They don't say anything except that they can't believe it, which they say again and again. What they do not believe, I want to not believe it with them. It's a helpful delusion if you can manage it. But I can't manage it. I can't make myself unbelieve the proof of my own eyes and what I know about my sister. This is one too many fantasies to uphold.

MUSIC FILTERS IN from a poolside boom box. It's Journey, "Don't Stop Believing." I am not making this up.

$$\rightarrow$$

When the homicide detective came to the hospital, where we waited in a close room furnished in mauve upholstery that was meant to be soothing but recalled instead a faded bruise, behind a door with a curtained window, he did not write anything down. He looked us in the eyes, all three of us at once. He was dressed casually, in a polo shirt and jeans. What did I expect? A dark suit? I pictured him leaving a cookout, handing the spatula to his younger brother. Here, you're the boss now, he said.

THE DETECTIVE BROUGHT his girlfriend with him, so the small-ness of the room became ridiculous, the stateroom for *A Night at the Opera.* I waited for the manicurist, for room service, for the maid. No, we don't want any; sure, come inside. The girlfriend wore a halter top and tight jeans. She may have been undercover at the cookout, waiting to catch someone in the act of eating undercooked meat. Her straight red hair was pulled back, leaving a thick fringe of bangs over her forehead, and she looked down and away when I stared at her face, as if she could hide behind these bangs, as if this would prevent me from seeing who she was and that she didn't belong in that room, which she didn't, since there was a sign on the outside that said "Family Room." Family Room is not like the one in your house where you watch *The Brady Bunch* and wonder why your family does not solve problems as neatly as one that combines the children of two divorces. (Or were they widowed? Why do we never see the pall of their previous marriages hanging over their relationship?) The Family Room is where they put you when something bad has happened to your family and you need to be kept away from everyone else, for your protection and the protection of others. A very small leper colony. A soundproof room on a game show, where contestants are forced to wait in silent tension. Except the Family Room is not silent, it's loud with anticipation and fear, because when we are permitted to leave this room, we will be ushered into the next phase of the contest, one for which we have received no preparation. What they don't tell you is that all the trials that came before this one, difficult as they seemed, will now be barely recognizable as life, like remnants from a quaint fantasy, a Norman Rockwell past. Now, you will say, this is life. Now I've received my scar. The people who don't have theirs yet, some of whom will escape with only surface contusions, seem to me of another race, an inferior one. They can't teach me anything.

➔

117

The first person I knew who did himself in was my grandmother's husband. Let's call him Marvin. That's a good grandmother's-husband name. No one in my generation is named Marvin and lives past junior high school to tell about it. So Marvin. I was at the wedding. He was not my actual grandfather. My grandmother was beautiful even when she was old and lots of people wanted to marry her, which may be why she got married lots of times. The time to Marvin, however, was the last time. Marvin was very fat, and I was too old to sit on his lap, but he insisted. I didn't know my real grandfather, and Marvin was going to sub in. At his behest and my grandmother's insistence—"Marvin asked you to sit on his lap, Miranda. Now be a good girl"—I balanced on his knee, his large belly pressing into my side, and watched him eat oranges. He ate the pulp, spit out the seeds, and then ate the rind, pith and all. That was when I knew that Marvin was not right in the head. I asked him, "Why do you eat the peel?"

He said, "I take the good with the bad, the nasty with the sweet, the ripe with the decayed." Even then I thought, shouldn't he say "the ripe with the green"? Decay is the wrong choice.

When Marvin showed me his penis in the bathroom later, all I could think was how small and sad it was, hanging there like the tip of the thumb of an empty glove half-hidden beneath his gut. When he asked me to touch it, I laughed. And then my grandmother said, "Marvin asked you to touch his penis, Miranda. Now be a good girl." No of course she didn't; she was in the next room kissing people and then wiping the lipstick off their cheeks. It was only later that I told on him, and by later I mean after he died, which was only a few months later, but not right after he died, not until now. I'm telling on him now.

WHY DID MARVIN pick me for this demonstration and not my

sister? Donna wasn't home that day, it's true; she was older and away at overnight camp. It didn't occur to me until after Donna died that Marvin may have given her a similar show, but that she simply never mentioned it, at least not to me. Maybe, like me, Donna only told someone who'd listen without protest. In which case, her poster of Peter Frampton holds many secrets, and I wish I could hear them. But why do I suspect that I was a more entertaining target for Marvin in the first place? Or simply that I was there.

I THINK MARVIN did it with pills. I found out he was what we then called manic-depressive. Now we say "bipolar," which sounds like we're talking about a world traveler. No one talked about his dying for more than a minute. Marvin went directly from being a name exclaimed with exuberance to a name that was only whispered, when it was uttered at all.

I FELT SILLY mentioning his penis when it could do me no further harm. I wasn't sure it had done me any harm in the first place. I knew only that something about the situation was off. At the time, I told someone I thought wouldn't judge me, that is, I told Julia the nurse, the tiny doll version of a black woman who was on TV. My dog had chewed off Julia's head, so it was a lot like telling no one. I went to my room and sat Headless Julia down and spoke in a serious voice to make sure I had her attention. I think I did a convincing impression of Marvin's belly using my pillow, with my thumb standing—no, sagging—in for his dick.

➔

In the Family Room, the detective's girlfriend smiled a sad-eyed apology for her presence, rather than for my sister. The detective's shirt was unbuttoned, and there were dark curls where his girlfriend put her lips. Later, my parents wouldn't remember her at all. If I insisted she was there, they'd agree just to shut me up. They remembered the detective, because he didn't listen to them when they said how my sister was happy, how my sister was fine, how all the trouble was long ago and over.

➤

Can I perform a pas de deux alone? I can leap; I can catch myself. Here I am, my sister and me, I'm both now. And neither. I bring my leg back down and stand on both feet on the balcony. I bend and right the wilted plant. I gather up the spilled soil with my hands, scraping my fingers on the rough concrete.

BAD SIDE IN

I'M DAYDREAMING ABOUT a white box truck.

And look, it has just pulled into my driveway. It could be the very
one they talked about last night on the news, the one we're supposed
to watch out for and worry about. Except, on the side of this truck
there's a picture of a horse, a bucking bronco, and in brown lettering
it says Mustang Fence. The horse reminds me of my son's pajamas.
My son, who's at school now, who for the first time didn't refuse to
get out of the car when I pulled up to the front of the carpool line,
who didn't complain when his sister reached over, as always without my permission, and unbuckled his seatbelt for him too soon,
before I'd even stopped at the curb. If she could, she'd shove him
out the door while the car's still moving, so eager is she to have him
utterly out of her life. I do understand this impulse, as I had a sister
once whom I sometimes thought to shove to her death, and then, by
the time I no longer thought of doing it, she went and did herself
in with no help from me at all. Which doesn't let me off the hook.
Funny how that works, that the dead keep on living in ways both
good and bad.

But as for the boy, to my amazement, this morning he didn't protest or whine, he simply got out of the car when he was supposed to, said "Bye," as if he'd been doing it for twenty years, like a man being dropped off for his daily ride on the commuter train into the city. He waved, he was gone. His sister slid across the seat and followed. And I came home to meet a man who'll build a fence around our yard, which I'm telling myself will keep the bad guys out and keep my children in.

A tall fence will at best deter the deer who mistake my backyard for Rock Creek Park, and at worst annoy my neighbors, with their split rail that won't stop a rabbit. As if they're on a ranch instead of our tidy enclave tucked between D.C.'s largest urban park and one of its primary avenues. Our sedate street lined with old oaks could trick you into thinking of suburbia. The detached houses are set farther apart than in some other neighborhoods, and it's mostly quiet. The traffic—commuters from the actual suburbs passing on their way to and from the business district—sounds more like the tides on a beach, dampened by the stately apartment buildings that overlook the avenue. But the trees' roots raise and crack the sidewalks, and their branches interfere with the power lines that crisscross among our neat brick houses like a botched game of cat's cradle. And the city, invisible though it may be from here, does come to us. The neighbors may like to imagine they're home on the range, but they've made one concession to reality—there are bars on their basement windows.

I care less about my neighbors and their country aspirations than I do about this: knowing we have a fence, and one that's as tall as I can make it, I'll feel like I've done something about circumstances that, when it comes down to it, I can't do anything about.

THE FENCE MAN has surprised me by arriving on time. I'm not prepared. I grab a dish towel with the hand that's not bleeding and wrap it around the one that I've just injured. I try to recall what the first-aid book says: elevate. In a few minutes, he'll walk into my kitchen, take a look around and say, "You've been busy."

When he emerges from his white box truck, carrying a clipboard and wearing a belt with the things contractors always have hanging off their belts—giant tape measure, Leatherman all-in-one, ratchet, cell phone swathed in what might double as a baseball glove—I decide he isn't a sniper or a criminal, probably, of any kind.

The neighbor's split rail runs along one side of our backyard. It's the only piece of fence that touches our property. Through the window, I watch the fence man examine a rotting post as if it might be an artifact from a previous civilization. What can he learn from the aging of pressure-treated pine? Rap on it once, I want to tell him, and the carpenter bees will hover anxiously above their holes. Rap on it twice, and you'll get a splinter. He's crouching over the place where it's buried in the ground. He rubs his chin, looks at his boots. He turns toward the house, and I duck away from the window.

A squirrel's sitting on the bird feeder platform, wolfing down sunflower seeds. I wish I had a BB gun. But I'm not known for my aim. I'd probably hit the fence guy himself, who's now bushwhacking among the azaleas to find the cinderblock property markers, which my daughter painted green "to go with the grass" and then plastered with American Girl stickers. I was sure these would wash away when it rained but they didn't.

I'm holding a roll of duct tape. I cut lengths of tape with scissors. I don't like the way the adhesive gums up the scissors; they stick together when I'm trying to cut. Does everything have to be difficult? I make a ball of duct tape and throw it at the squirrel in the feeder. The ball hits the window, sticks for a second, and falls into the sink. The squirrel jumps down but another takes its place. I think of a rigged carnival game, the squirrel ducking at the last possible moment. But the squirrels are too far away, a coward's distance for shooting. I can't see their eyes.

THE FENCE MAN has disappeared. Moments later, the doorbell rings. I open the front door, and he doesn't look up immediately, because he's busy punching the keys on a calculator with the eraser end of his pencil. He puts the calculator in his front pocket, tucks the clipboard under his arm, sticks his hand out and says, "Vince Palomino."

When I called to request an estimate, was it Misty of Chincoteague who took down my name and address? But Misty of Chincoteague is sitting on a shelf in my daughter's bedroom. I don't mean the book, although that's there, too; I'm thinking of the model horse itself, which I saved for twenty years in case I ever had a daughter. Secretariat's also gathering dust, along with an unnamed Appaloosa mare and colt, and yes, of course, a mustang, in a color the model horse people call "buckskin." The mustang is frozen in mid-gallop and perched on a stand so it doesn't tip over. These models belonged to me when I was almost the same age my daughter is now, when I was obsessed with horses like every girl that age. This obsession lasts until you discover boys, a fact that requires no explanation.

When I was still horse-obsessed, I took riding lessons in which we shuffled around a muddy ring on tired steeds beaten down and broken by the oppressive affections of little girls. The languid indifference in the way my horse took a chunk of carrot from my hand with its velvet lip and the edge of its teeth, the way it rolled its eyes away from me when I grabbed its nose to pet it, the way it shook its head up and down, trying to free itself when I held its bridle and stroked its haunch, these ways that a horse didn't care about me, about any of us nine-year-old girls, this prepared me for life. Because there would always be that effort, wasted effort, to capture the wandering eye of that world-weary, ambivalent horse.

VINCE PALOMINO COCKS his head at me. I see the powerful tendons in the curve of his neck, a bit of gray sprouting from beneath the top button of his chambray shirt. There's something guileless in his expression, probably misleading. He's slope-shouldered and stocky. I can see the shape of him through his shirt and the thighs of his blue jeans where they're faded almost to white. I'm liking the idea of watching him dig post holes. The backs of his hands are furred blond.

He removes his heavy lace-up boots on entering my foyer. There they are in the corner, tongues hanging out.

When he says his name and holds out a hand toward me, I stare at it for a second too long before putting out my own hand—"Miranda Weber," I say—and then remember I'm holding a blood-soaked dish towel. His business smile changes into a look that can only be described as "This woman expects me to shake her bloody hand," but a moment later there's a considered shift to "Is this what I need to do to sell a fence?" He reaches out, and I pull back my hand as in a gag, sub in my left hand at the last second, both of us obviously relieved.

"I had an accident," I say. With a can of beans. I don't say that.

"Are you all right?" he says. I can tell he means it in more than one way. "Do you have a bandage?"

"Let's go in here," I say. I notice him noticing the pile of emergency blankets I dumped in the living room. I say, cheerily, "Kids, making forts!" Why say anything? I always feel that I owe an explanation. Why? Once I begin to explain, the other party decides that in fact I do need to explain—and by "other party" I mean "husband"—and that my explanation is insufficient. And then we argue. This happens all the time. That's just what marriage is, at least what it is now, after ten years, a constant stream of insufficient explaining. It's hard work coming up with all of these explanations. That's what people mean when they say "marriage takes work." That, and settling on whether the toilet paper should peel off the roll from the front or from the back.

I lead Vince Palomino past the blankets to the kitchen, to the table, where he can sit and tell me how much this fence will cost. That's when he looks around the room and says, "You've been busy." It sounds like he's saying, "Should I come back later?"

Maybe it was a mistake to bring him into the kitchen, but the dining room table is the setting for my kids' art projects, my son's orange construction paper jack-o-lantern, and my daughter's half-finished White House made of grass clippings, cotton, and glue. The kitchen table is clear except for the scattered balls of duct tape, which I now brush into one of the boxes I carried up from the basement earlier.

"I'm sorry for the mess, I was going through something. Some boxes."

Vince appears unfazed. He's not really looking at me though, because who'd look at me closely in my current condition? Besides the bloody hand, there's my Land's End mom uniform, the stretch-waist jeans—that pregnancy weight hanging in well post-pregnancy—and my loosely draping T-shirt which at least conveys that I have breasts, even if it says nothing detailed about them.

He seems to be waiting for me to say something. If he asked me a question I didn't hear it. I look at him dumbly, at his dark blue eyes, dirty-blond hair. He's older than me by about ten years, I'm guessing. Thick eyebrows, several shades darker than his hair, meet in the middle. He sits down.

"I just moved, myself," says Vince. "Unpacking's a bear. Let my wife do that, too."

He's not wearing a wedding band. "Do you have kids, Mr. Palomino?"

"Call me Vince," he says. "No, no kids. Working on it." He smiles in a way that's both wistful and conveys that at least it's fun working on it.

"That's tough," I say. "Good luck." Good luck? Like he's playing the lottery?

"You have . . . three? . . ." he says.

It would be easy to make that mistake, given the piles of twigs around the yard that my son calls "houses for Eeyore," the Matchbox cars embedded in the mulch, and the fingerprint smudges on the walls.

"Just two," I say. "A boy and a girl."

"A complete set," says Vince. "How old?"

"Four and eight. My daughter's eight," I say.

"My nephews are eight. Twins," says Vince. "My sister has her hands full."

My hand's full of blood. I squeeze the towel around it in my lap. My sister didn't have kids. And she didn't know my kids; my son hadn't even been born when she died, and my daughter was only a baby. "Twins. Busy household," I say. It's what you say.

"When I call her, they're always on her for something," says Vince. "'Play with me.' 'Look at me!' She can never talk."

I like Vince. He's trying to make babies but he's not sure if he wants them. A healthy apprehensiveness. "Yeah, that's frustrating," I say. "But on the other hand it's nice to be—" I almost say "needed." "—when they still want to play with you. They get to make the rules, and they think it's funny when you mess up." I stop suddenly, conscious that I'm about to blather on.

He fingers his tape measure where it hangs from his belt, draws the tape out and back, out and back. I note the twitching of muscle in his downy forearm. "Seems like, I don't know how you ever get it right," he says.

He's talking about something else. I want to tell him he's right about that much. Everything becomes what my son calls a "redo." You have to be forgiven, again and again. But I just say, "Yeah, I know what you mean." And then I say, "You know, when you drove up in the white truck—that was alarming." I laugh to show that I'm not actually alarmed. Or, alarming.

"Oh yeah," he says. "Needle in a haystack isn't it? Crazy—stuff." He's looking at a streak of red crayoned up my forearm. I don't think it was there before.

"Yeah, crazy," I say.

"It's an awfully tall fence you want," he says. "You have a dog?"

"No, no dog," I say. "Not yet," I add, because I need his approval.

"Well, now you can get one," he says. "A big one."

"Exactly. That's what I want, a big dog. My kids'll like that." He knows I'm talking in code. He knows why I want the fence.

"Why don't I work this out," he points at the estimate sheet, "and you go take care of that." He bobs his Palomino head toward my arm. His forehead's creased in a way that gives him a permanent look of empathy. "You should take care of that."

"It's nothing," I say. "A flesh wound." That's what I'll say to my husband later. "A flesh wound." It's a film reference that he knows. I hope he'll laugh. Devin's laugh is one reason why I married him. When he's laughing with me, I know he's remembering what we are when we're at our best. In those moments, I can forget what I need to forget and remember only the way he labored with our daughter to build a solar-powered radio for the science fair, and how, when it failed to pick up a signal, he reassured her that even for adults, designs don't always work the way we intended.

Vince doesn't get my joke. He squints at me like I've spoken in a foreign language and he's trying to read the subtitles.

➔

My husband was held up at gunpoint once, the same year Mayor Barry said that the incidence of crime in D.C. was quite low, "if you take out the killings." It happened before we met. A boy came out of the shadows and asked, "Does Whitey want to know what a gun looks like? Should I bring it closer?"

ALL THE MAJOR roads in D.C. lead to traffic circles, eventually. Once you reach a circle, you're forced to make important decisions in a matter of seconds. Which lane to take, and, once you're in the circle, which exit is the correct one and how to get over to it. Nothing's marked, or not well-marked. If you don't know what to do or where to go, you'll cause an accident. If you don't know how to drive around a circle, the safest option is to keep going around and going around until you figure it out. If you stop going around, you'll be hit. You can't stop. L'Enfant intended for these circles to be destinations; instead they're obstacles.

I TRY NOT to think of the gun and of my husband's frightened face. I can't think of him that way. It's wrong, but I need to think of him as invulnerable. Which, no one is, in case the news of the day—of every day—hasn't made that perfectly clear. And yet he wasn't shot, and we did meet, and we had children. And he's not here. I keep going around the circle; I'm not sure I'll ever get off.

➔

I leave Vince in the kitchen and search upstairs for Band-Aids. How did it happen that there are no Band-Aids in the emergency supply box, when we thought of everything else? We followed the official guidelines to the letter. I put my hand under running water and watch the blood circle the drain. There's a jagged cut below my middle finger, traveling toward the center of my palm, just missing what I believe to be the important vein between my thumb and forefinger, the vein that might have sent me to the emergency room. My daughter cut herself in that spot last year.

My daughter has no interest in horses, model or otherwise. So why do I press them on her, surprising her every few months with a "new" one from among the boxes I still keep in the basement? What does she like if not horses? Why don't I know?

My daughter looks very much like a girl in my riding class. Sally Jenkins; blonde, blue-eyed, rosy-cheeked, and freckled. Sally wore a pristine velvet helmet she brought with her to class and shiny black riding boots. I was one of the few who borrowed a battered helmet, supplied by the stables for kids who didn't have their own.

This scuffed helmet looked like the one the boy in my sister's special ed class wore so he could safely bang his head against the wall. He did this randomly throughout the day, rocked and banged his head. No one seemed to know why he did it. Donna was upset by his behavior, and when she was upset, she paced back and forth, staring at the floor and muttering to herself. It was quite a scene, the boy banging and rocking, my sister pacing, muttering. Eventually our parents took Donna out of that school and put her in one where she could be with normal kids for some of her classes. That was supposed to be a good thing, but I think that's when she started to realize she wasn't normal.

I remembered the boy every time I put on that helmet at the start of riding class. I thought of what it might feel like to bang my head against a wall.

MY SISTER GOT out of this, I catch myself thinking. I hate her, just a little bit, for being dead. All her worries, over.

I FIND SOME gauze but no tape. I fix the gauze to my palm with Spiderman Band-Aids and hope it'll hold.

When I return, Vince is standing at the stove peering under the lid of the large stockpot I left there. I catch him with a certain look on his face, like he's not sure if he might find human fingers boiling in the pot.

"Sorry—I smelled something burning," he says. His lips are drawn back, exposing his top teeth. The bottom edges of his teeth are flat-tened and almost even across the length of his smile: he grinds his teeth in his sleep. Is he, too, dreaming of shooters and sinister box trucks unlike his own, and powdery substances that arrive by mail and shoes with built-in fuses and other hazards of modern living? Or are his fears more concrete—that his wife won't get pregnant, or that she will?

He yields the stove to me. I thought I left the pot on simmer, but the burner is bright red, as if it's embarrassed to have anything to do with this meal. I turn it down to low and stir the contents, which have stuck to the bottom. It does smell like something's burning. "It'll be okay," I say. Because I have to believe it.

SALLY JENKINS RODE a horse named Finesse, a big black gelding. They were all geldings; we just didn't know it then. In a few weeks we'd be eligible to advance to the next level, to a jumping class. We were trotting in our fixed circle, what I now believe the horses must have understood as their personal circle of hell. Sally was straight in the stirrups, posting in perfect rhythm. She belonged on the cover of one of the horsemanship magazines they displayed on a hay bale outside the stable office. I pictured her there with a blue ribbon in her hand.

I couldn't post like Sally. My posting was slow, arrhythmic, graceless. I was never sure, was I going up too far or not far enough? Was it supposed to feel like this, the horse's wide, solid back whacking me, despite my ample padding, on the tailbone and the inner thighs? Was this what it should feel like? I asked myself nine years later, on my back on the narrow dorm-room mattress, squeaking springs spreading gossip before the boy would even leave the room to tell his friends. The answer to that one, it got better. When it was over he still carried the photo of his old girlfriend in his wallet, the girlfriend who dumped him the day before I met him at the college bar. I didn't know then about rebounds, and he didn't know about boundaries. Now I've had time to understand, though I never did advance to jumping, or I might know how to get over the fence I'm about to build to wall myself in.

WHEN IT CAME time to kick the horses into a canter, Sally tapped Finesse with her heels, clicked with her mouth, flicked the reins, but the horse didn't change his gait. She was two horses ahead of me, and when I saw her begin to smack Finesse on his flank with the riding crop and urge him to "Go boy, go Finesse," I could see the red splotches on her cheeks that matched the strain in her voice. The horse still didn't cooperate. Instead, ignoring the rules of the circle, he came to a complete and sudden halt. Those of us behind were forced to swerve out of line to avoid bowling each other over. Finesse dropped to his knees. To her credit, Sally hung on as her horse folded its legs underneath itself in the dirt, as if it had given up. Sally continued to hang on as Finesse rolled onto his side, crushing her right leg beneath his body. I heard her still calling, through her sobs, for him to get up and go, Finesse, go. The instructors ran into the ring to try and extract her from under the horse, while the rest of us stood around gawping. They sent us away at a walk to the indoor ring near the barn. How badly was Sally hurt? I don't know. A girl in our class said she was in the hospital. I asked my mother if I could visit her, but she wouldn't take me. She said only family was allowed. I wrote Sally a card instead. I drew a picture of a horse on the front. Maybe that was a mistake. I never heard from her. I never saw Sally again. It would be nice if there had been a neat resolution, but that's not the way the world operates.

"CHILI?" SAYS VINCE. He's talking about what's in the pot.

"Goulash," I say. In my head, I've been calling this concoction Emergency Goulash. Inspired as it was by the government's official list, still available somewhere on something-dot-gov. In accordance with the government's instructions to everyone last year, we gathered supplies like we were on a scavenger hunt. What store still has a crank radio in stock? You have to order it online. Where to find the best child-size gas masks? The Israeli Army supplier—everyone knows that. There's a list for a "basic emergency," and a list for sheltering in place, a list for what to keep in your car and what to keep in your office. We followed all of these advisories to the letter, as if they were for prevention, rather than a lame and insufficient response to something potentially deadly that, when these stored items actually come into play, will have already occurred, and at which time we'll be lucky to survive long enough to find a use for any of them. I see a future of duct tape-based children's games, developed while in hiding from a chemical attack, a 9/11 version of the original "Ring around the Rosie," which not enough people know is really about everyone dying from Plague.

But this isn't what we thought about last year. We prepared for an emergency with optimistic busyness and a sense of accomplishment. We kept these supplies stored faithfully, in the belief that we were doing something useful and proactive. Back then, the magical properties of duct tape hit their highest levels of potency. Fill a room with duct tape, close the door, forget about it for six months, no, a year. If you can. And it worked, because in that time, Nothing Happened. Almost nothing.

Now, the protective talismans in our house have stopped working. The enemy adapts. Now, it's considered a sane course of action to use one's car as a shield, to hide in the back seat and shrink down below window-level while gas—but you hope not a bullet—pumps into your car. Because for weeks now, an anonymous sniper with no apparent motive has been shooting at people, people who have nothing in common besides their subsequent appearance on the evening news—except that some of them were pumping gas at the time. How would that feel, I wonder, to know that you're going to die at a gas station? Or, as one man did, while waiting for the Metrobus. En route, always en route, never arriving. Keep going around the circle. Don't stop for anything.

The other night, the news warned us to be on the lookout for a white box truck. Then another murder, which I lived and relived as I walked up the driveway reading the morning paper on a street lined with white box trucks, the favorite vehicle of contractors. Out my door, every morning, a waiting death squad in the shade of the oaks.

The hoarded emergency supplies—to what purpose in this case? If only the game show *Let's Make a Deal* were still on the air. I always wanted to be on that show, to be the woman Monty Hall calls on because she can produce a can of asparagus from inside her purse. *I have asparagus, Monty!* I'd shout and wave the can in the air. And when he picked me I'd jump up and down in complete abandonment of my dignity—*Here! in my purse! I have it!* He'd give me a choice: Curtain Number 1, Number 2, Number 3. Behind one of these curtains, he'd tell me, I might be lucky enough to find a new car or a washer-dryer or a trip to San Francisco! And I'd choose Curtain Number 2. The curtain would open to reveal a goat chewing grass.

Left with this canned bounty, this smorgasbord of paranoia, some might throw up their hands. Instead, I make goulash. Instead, I'll put up a fence. I want the theoretical, legal borders of our property to be physical and visible. And I can't wrap my yard in duct tape, though I wonder if this is a project Christo would consider. What's he done since he finished the Reichstag, anyway?

"BAD SIDE OUT?" Vince has been talking. I haven't heard any of it. He looks up from his papers.

"I'm sorry," I say. "Would you mind repeating that?"

"Sure. How about a picture?" He draws in pencil on the back of his estimate form. "Here's what the bad side looks like," he says. "It's the side we'll build the fence from, because we need to assemble it here, you see, screws here and there." He's made a picture of a section of fence that shows the horizontal supports crossing the planks.

"It's not bad," I say.

"It's like seeing an X-ray, versus seeing the same person wearing clothes," he says.

I don't think that's an apt comparison, but I don't argue with Vince. He could be talking about me and my clothes. I look better with them on.

"The good side looks like this," he says. He sketches some more.

"Oh, pretty," I say. No skeleton showing. Just smooth vertical planks connected to posts with neat crowns on top.

"Yeah, the clean side," he says. "If we do it facing out, good side facing your neighbors, we build it from inside your yard. If it's bad side out, we build it from the neighbors' side, from their yard."

"What do most people do?"

"Easy," says Vince. "Bad side in."

"Of course," I say. Who wants their neighbors to see their bad side?

"It's not just for looks," he says. "The bad side is easy to climb, so if you face it out, people can climb over the fence and into your yard. It's like leaving a ladder lying around."

Vince Palomino wants to save me from harm—from leaving ladders around, from nimble thieves, from bleeding to death. "That *is* bad," I say. "Bad side in, it is."

Vince wrinkles his nose. The asparagus; I smell it now, too. I know it doesn't belong in a pot with canned tomatoes and assorted beans and button mushrooms. But I couldn't have it in the house, not for one more day. What if canned asparagus, my secret weapon, had kept the terrorists at bay for the past year? I imagine them entering my house right now with their nefarious plans and then changing their minds because of what they smell simmering on the stove, Osama's lieutenant saying how he hates the way his pee smells when he eats asparagus. On the other hand, who gets asparagus in those mountain caves in Afghanistan? Maybe they'd be willing to negotiate for a delicacy such as this. "Let's make a deal," I'd say to Osama. "You stay on the good side of the fence, while we live on the bad side."

VINCE PUSHES AWAY from the table and stands. "I think we should go outside," he says. "Some things to show you."

"Okay." I get the key and unlock the back door, leaving a smear of blood on the doorknob; it's coming through the bandage. Elevate it. I should have elevated it.

"Remember to call Miss Utility," says Vince, as we cross the lawn. "If the utilities aren't marked, we can't do any work."

He thinks he's got the job. He hasn't given me a price yet.

We walk to the other side, where the gate will be. He talks about options, shows me a brochure with pictures of different kinds of gates and what he calls "hardware." He stomps the dirt and dust flies up. He shakes his head and points to the chrysanthemums, which are still in bloom, late. "You'll have to move those," he says.

"It won't kill them?" I say.

"Ma'am, I'm no gardener." I got the "ma'am" treatment. I'm toast. I'm invisible.

"Better check with your garden store," he says.

I almost hope digging up the mums will kill them. They don't know when to let go. To me, they've always been ugly, the color of rust. In a week or two they'll turn dry and brown at the edges, their faces crumpling in like the mouths of toothless old men.

Vince looks at his watch. He's losing patience with me. I missed a signal somewhere.

BEFORE PALOMINO RODE in on his white horse, I awoke sweating over box trucks, and then the new shooting, and the idea that we had a closet full of plastic sheeting cut precisely to cover the windows and vents in case of a chemical attack and many gallons of bottled water and canned beans and a crank radio to ensure we'd be informed of escape routes and current conditions, and duct tape, loads of duct tape—I wanted to get rid of it all, and I wanted to have a talk with the people who told me I needed to buy it in the first place.

When Vince, whom I didn't yet know as Vince, pulled into the driveway, I took a panicked look around my kitchen, at the wasteland of supplies that I'd half unpacked, at the sloppy cans standing empty on the countertop, lids open like mouths, at the large pot of disappointment I'd just started on the stove. I began rinsing the cans and tossing them into the recycle bin. I cut myself on one of the razor-sharp lids.

"YOU MAY WANT to rethink the birdseed," says Vince, as we go back inside. "You're providing a constant food supply for rats."

"I am," I say. It's not a question. It all fits together. Build a fence, bad side in, and this teeming disaster of my yard and my house and the world will be contained; what belongs inside will stay inside the square box. The bad can escape, and once it's all gone it cannot climb back inside. Good.

Vince hands me his estimate. I look at it but I don't really look at it. "Okay," I say.

"You sure?" he says.

"Yes." He shows me where to sign the estimate. I sign it.

"Why don't you keep it and call me," he says. "Mr. Weber might want to take a look, no?" He doesn't believe me. He knows I can write a check that my husband might cancel. This has happened to Vince before. And he keeps calling my husband Weber, which is my last name but not his; I don't correct him.

"I'm good for it," I say.

I watch him leave. He gets into his truck and shoves his copy of my signed estimate into the crevice between the dashboard and the windshield, where there are a lot of other papers and an empty Styrofoam cup and a box from Dunkin' Donuts.

ON THE NEWS that night I learn that Saddam Hussein has been reelected by one hundred percent of Iraqi voters. And yet, he has many doubles. They're seen climbing into identical black cars in which they ride serpentine around Baghdad, while the real Hussein may be far away in Paris or Amsterdam or Moscow or Buenos Aires.

The same broadcast reveals that a witness has cast doubt on the white box truck theory. It seems the police have been led astray. My husband says that on the Clara Barton Parkway, police stop every third vehicle, shining a flashlight through the open window, searching the inside. Now any car is suspect.

In the grocery line, the checker says, "With a mustache they all look alike anyway. May as well kill all of them, just to be sure."

⇥

"Look at me!" my daughter's shouting. She performs a maneuver called "skin the cat," something I once knew how to do myself. She practiced for days—falling, bruises, scraped palms—and now she finally has it. With both hands, she hangs onto a low branch of the oak that grows on our neighbor's front lawn. She bends her knees and brings them up and through the open space created between her arms and the branch. When she's upside down, her head toward the ground, her long hair brushing the dry leaves there, she lets go of the branch, completing the motion, a backward somersault almost in midair. She drops to the ground, landing on her feet. I stand in the grass and watch her do it again and again and again. I think of Sally Jenkins, who wouldn't give up even when she was about to be crushed. My daughter's grip on the branch is sure. She swings her feet up and through, her body turns over itself, and her landing is solid, an imitation of a Russian gymnast. Every time, I cheer for her. She looks up at me with an eager, serious face, and waits. I raise my fists and open them to reveal her score: a ten.

The cut on my palm is beginning to scab over; the bandage holds.

THREAT POTENTIAL

THAT OTHER TIME she was in Mexico there was a swim-up bar. She posed in a bikini and entered a contest; she hadn't felt demeaned, just pretty. She was thicker around the middle now, and she wouldn't wear a bikini. She looked like what she was: A 39-year-old mother of two. It had happened overnight. And, it had taken forever.

This time they'd eschewed the resort for a rental. They were supposed to be independent, unlike the hordes of cruise-ship debarkees. They were supposed to reduce the barriers between their family and an authentic experience, introduce the kids to another culture, that was the idea. No Gipsy Kings blaring from a boom box; no midday margaritas. Even the vendors who hawked their wares on the tourist beaches didn't come this far down the coastline. Why should vacation have to mean insulation? Her husband had said that.

They'd rented half of a duplex from a retired Scandinavian; she wasn't sure which country he was from. They had the right side of the duplex—stucco walls, clay tile floors, oversized chairs and sofas the color of earth and sun, mirrors with interesting hammered metal frames. She wondered what his side was like. Was he having an authentic experience?

The other time she was in Mexico no one had to be reminded to avoid rinsing with tap water when brushing their teeth, or to avoid drinking the shower water, and in fact no one had dropped a toothbrush in the toilet then, either. But there were no children then. They were different people when they took that trip. There was no husband; there was no wife. There was still a sister.

Besides the tap water, there was an abstract risk to this location. There had been a murder a mile down the beach. Three coves down. The coves were separated by rocky outcroppings and piles of dead bleached coral. They'd been told not to be concerned about the crime. It was unusual. It was a drug thing, not a crime against tourists. Not specifically, even though the victims, a young couple, they were tourists. They were mixed up in something, that was the consensus. They were beheaded. But that had nothing to do with her. There were burglaries; that was normal. Don't leave your camera on the beach, the books told you. Don't leave it on a table in plain sight in your kitchen while you're in the ocean, they said. Lock it up. Lock it all up. Most of the homes had guard dogs. Their house didn't have a dog, though in the husband's opinion children could be a deterrent, their behavior erratic and unpredictable when criminals liked to be able to predict.

It was the second day of their trip. The duplex had no pool, but she didn't think it necessary with the ocean twenty steps off the patio. The girl had taken a kayak and paddled out into the shallow water. The mother wished she wouldn't go alone. The boy played in the sand.

"Take a walk down the beach and look for coral with me," the father said.

"There's coral right here," the boy told him. "There are crabs in shells." He lined up the crabs and watched them creep like drunks. "Ready, set, go."

The father asked the mother to walk with him.

"I can't leave him alone," she said. "Maybe later."

"He's fine," the father said, and watched the boy for a moment as he turned a crab over and its feet raced silently in the air.

She looked from the boy in the sand to the ocean, where the daughter ventured ever farther from shore in the kayak, and told the father again, Maybe later. He picked up a plastic pail and walked off down the beach. She watched him stop and bend at the waist to pluck something from the sand. He turned it over, whatever it was, and put it in the pail. He kept walking, slowly. She watched him get smaller. She realized she hadn't been watching the girl. To her relief, she saw her daughter dragging the kayak up the beach, stepping around the sharp coral camouflaged in the sand. She was purposeful and only a little awkward, her legs still too long for her body. She'd grow into them. She was almost eleven. She stopped halfway and left the kayak, watched a brown pelican drop from the sky in a dive that incised the water's surface but left no scar. In a moment, the bird was floating on the waves, its bill drained of water.

"How do they see their food from up there?" the girl said.

"They must have good eyesight," the mother said.

"To see through the water?"

"I don't know," said the mother. "Maybe they only see a silhouette. But they know what they're looking for."

The boy said, "What if they make a mistake? What if they dive into the water and hit their head on something?"

"Whoever heard of a pelican hitting its head?" said the girl.

"What if there was an anchor stuck in the water that looked like a fish?" said the boy.

"Oh my god," said the girl. "It's not a cartoon."

"That's a good question," said the mother. "It can't only be shaped like a fish. It has to move like a fish. The bird has to be sure."

"I'm hungry," said the girl and stomped toward the house, kicking up sand.

"It's important to know what to look for," said the mother.

"Can we go to the ruins today?" said the girl.

The mother looked out from the patio over the Gulf. There were thin waterfalls of rain dropping out of faraway clouds. "See that? It looks like rain," she said. "We should wait for a clear day. It won't be nice in the rain."

"It rains every day," said the father. "For a little while."

"I don't want to go to the ruins in the jungle," said the boy. "I want to go to the snorkeling lagoon."

"We'll do that, too," said the father.

"He's afraid of the jungle," said the girl.

"Hey," said the mother.

"I'm not!" he said. "It's boring."

"There are spiders in the jungle as big as your head. That's not boring," said the girl.

"Not helpful," said the father.

That night the mother and father sat on the patio in a swing made of heavy rope, like a hammock. The waves were going and coming. The children were in the house. The girl was sleeping; the boy played solitaire on the tile floor.

"Do you want to come out here?" said the mother.

"Let him be," said the father. "We're finally alone."

"Yes," said the mother. "But solitaire?"

"Everyone should know how to be alone," said the father.

"Of course," said the mother. "But this is a family vacation. And he's seven."

"I'm forty-four," said the father.

"You look younger," said the mother, stroking the wiry hair on his knee. "But you look older than seven."

"I'm getting a beer." He stood and the swing's netting closed up around the mother's sides like an animal trap hidden in the sand. She was almost surprised she wasn't caught up and dangling from a tree.

"Want one?" he said, lining up the latest empty bottle with the others against the wall of the house.

"I'll have a sip of yours," she said.

He went inside.

"How's the game?" she heard him ask.

"I won," said the boy. "I'm playing again."

"Going for two out of three?" said the father. "Okay, but in five minutes you need to go to bed." She heard the door of the fridge open and close and the bottle cap clink to the floor when he popped it off with the opener that was screwed to the wall.

"Five minutes," he said. "Did you hear?"

"What?" said the boy.

"You're sister's already asleep."

"She's not playing cards," said the boy.

"She had a busy day in the water," said the father. "It made her tired. You'd be tired too if you did something besides dig and play with crabs."

"Daddy, I'm concentrating."

"Now it's four minutes."

"Please! Let me finish this game," said the boy. "Just this one game."

"I'm not playing this game again," said the father.

The mother listened, leaning forward with her feet flat on the ground, her hands squeezing the thick rope at the front edge of the swing as if she were about to get up, but she didn't.

The father returned. He handed her a beer, he'd brought two, and sat down. The mother's side of the swing lifted and opened again, and she floated, almost weightless.

"Look at those stars," he said. "Can't see that at home." It sounded the same as when he told the boy to go to bed.

The sky's infinity began to frighten her. She looked away.

"I knew you'd have more than a sip," he said.

"Who did that?" she said. Her bottle was almost empty.

"Enjoy yourself," said the father. "We're on vacation."

THE NEXT DAY, he said, "Look, it's clear. I think we can go today."

The mother shaded her eyes with her hand and made a show of gazing into the distance. "It's very hot," she said. "It's always worse inland. Maybe snorkeling . . ."

"Of course it's hot," said the father. "It wasn't my idea to come here this time of year." He paced away down the beach as if he might walk to the ruin on his own. "Just because the school break—"

Go ahead, thought the mother, throw a tantrum; blame the air.

He stopped and turned around. "It's the most impressive ruin outside of Tikal," said the father. "I refuse to miss it." He came close and whispered, "Kids are adaptable."

He was right. The mother knew he was right. Even though she suspected that in another day, the boy would be used to the idea. She couldn't help wanting to give him a chance to get used to it. She didn't say anything.

"Let's go snorkeling," said the boy. "I want to see a barracuda."

"Are there barracudas in the lagoon?" said the girl, sounding more curious than concerned.

"No," said the father. "The sharks scared them away."

$$\Rightarrow$$

They went to the ruins. "We should've started earlier," said the father. "We'll be walking in the heat of the day." In the car, he stared stiffly ahead, seldom blinking, gripping the steering wheel like a prisoner holding the bars on his cell.

Would she remember that later? Yes she would. What she couldn't quite remember was before. What did he remember of before? Before she'd disappointed him in some intangible way. Before her vigilance had ruined his pleasure. It wasn't always like this. He used to—when they were riding in the car, he used to put his right hand on her leg, stroke her leg, keep his hand there the whole way, as if to remind her that they were connected. And sometimes she'd unzip his fly and reach into his pants and feel him warm up under her fingers. Sometimes, she convinced him to pull over and move into the back seat with her, or to recline so that she could take him in her mouth. Thinking about this, she put her hand on his bare thigh and kept it there. His neck turned pink, but he didn't look at her until a minute passed, and then he warned her, without speaking, with a glance at her hand. They still had that language, that language of looks. She moved her hand away.

They bought Cokes made with real sugar from a vendor in the parking lot.

"It's not real sugar at home?" said the girl.

"Corn syrup," said the father. "It doesn't taste as good."

"Can I have another," said the boy. "Please?"

"One's enough," said the father.

"But we're on vacation," said the boy. "Please?"

The mother wondered if he'd heard his father say that the night before.

"We didn't come here for Cokes. Look around you," said the father. "We're lucky. Most people never see places like this."

Like the parking lot? the mother thought.

The boy began blowing across the open mouth of the Coke bottle, making annoying sounds that ranged from "wort" and "worrrrt" to "wert" and even "werrrrt." The mother did her best to ignore it; she could tell the father was doing the same.

"Let's put on bug repellent before we go into the woods," she said, pulling the spray bottle out of her bag. "Hold still," she told the girl.

"Can't we go—let's go," said the girl.

"One sec." The mother sprayed her daughter's legs, took the girl's hat and sprayed it, then put it back on her head. The mother could see, peripherally, her husband watching with his hands on his hips.

It was hard to keep from rating everything according to its threat potential when you had kids. Especially considering what her own sister had done—the deep suspicion that what had happened to her sister had been predictable and yet was not predicted, this still haunted her.

The mother would make an excellent Homeland Security analyst. Sizing up every variable. She did this constantly, without trying. Some threats couldn't be managed or prevented. This didn't mean she stopped thinking about them.

When she was freed, the girl said, "I want to see the pyramid. I'm climbing all the way up."

"Good for you," said the father.

"Werrrt," went the boy.

The densely wooded entrance opened onto a wide dirt road. Tour guides were gathered there, waiting to give visitors a lift in wheeled carts pulled by bicycles.

"Can you believe they do that in this heat?" said the mother. They weren't even wearing hats.

Her husband spoke to one of the men. "He says it's a half-hour walk to the main cluster of ruins and another fifteen minutes to the pyramid."

The boy read from a laminated map tacked to a tree: "*You are on the white road. This road was made by Mayan people. It's called white because it's made out of limestone. It can be seen in the dark.*"

"Let's go in a cart," said the girl, tugging on the mother's arm.

"Makes sense," the father said. "We'll go directly to the center and work our way out from there."

They split up and sat two and two in the carts, she with her daughter. The road was bumpy—pockmarked, rutted, washboard. With each bump, the cart gave a sharp bounce, and where the mother felt it in her spine and spent half the ride with her teeth clenched in preparation for the pain, the girl let out a cry of happy fear, like she was on a rollercoaster. The mother forgot the pain and instead remembered a time when she'd been that way, when the ordinary world seemed packed with unexpected sources of delight. All parents want to freeze such a moment when they see it in their child— the moment in which everything seems, not perfect but imperfectly right, full of an imperfect happiness, displayed as it was because the girl wasn't old enough yet to be too embarrassed to behave that way. Some girls her age might be. And for this, the mother was in pain again because this imperfect perfection was already shifting the very moment she noticed it, like a needle on a vinyl record slipping off the hump between grooves. Because when you recognize that you're in such a moment, it's already gone.

And then the mother realized that in fact she couldn't remember being in that state herself—the state that her daughter seemed to live in—more than a handful of times. The first one that came to her, same as a jolt in the spine, was when the French boy kissed her, when they hid in a closet at a nightclub in Paris and kissed until their tongues were swollen and their lips were raw. She was sixteen and was drunk only on that kiss. It happened again, but it was never the same way, and then his parents insisted he give her up. It was like peeling off a layer of her skin. There were other times, too, which she recounted to herself, jolting herself as the cart jolted, as her daughter cried out and laughed. It struck her that most of the moments that came to mind were about sex. Those were the times she could forget herself. Her body would force her mind into submission rather than the other way around. Is that the only way? She was always anticipating, preparing for something—another more perfect point in time. The next hurdle to go before that elusive period of stasis. (Stasis, as a goal, seemed overrated only to people without children.) She told herself it was practical and necessary. She told herself that living in the moment was fine for children and for the otherwise irresponsible. But now she wondered if this wasn't all terribly sad.

There were fewer bumps now; they must be getting closer to the goal. They passed half-hidden structures no more assuming than mounds of stones overgrown with weeds. It can't have been an accident that this place was found; someone knew what to look for. The girl made a game of spotting the ruins from a distance. Some of them were camouflaged with dirt and sod, while others had been partially unearthed. The mother had read that the ruin was vast, and in a continual state of excavation, but it was something else to see the evidence. The past rising up from under the dirt and breaking into the present.

"There it is," said her daughter, nearly standing up in the cart. "I can see the tippy top above those trees."

"Good eye," said the mother.

"I want to be an explorer," said the daughter. "Like Indiana Jones. I want to discover a place no one has ever seen."

"I think you will," said the mother. One of the best things about being a kid was that everything was a discovery. Why did that have to end?

"I can't wait, I can't wait," said her daughter, and as soon as the cart stopped, she hopped out without help. She stood on tiptoe and jumped up and down, trying to see beyond the tall trees.

The guide pointed to a path taken over by giant ferns and told the mother it was a few minutes' walk to the pyramid. Now that the clatter of the ride had ended, she heard new sounds—whirring and chirping and, at unpredictable intervals, a distant whoop.

"What's that? *Qué es esto*?" She cupped a hand on her ear to mean "sounds." Her Spanish was now rudimentary and embarrassing, when once she was fluent. She'd won an award in school.

"What is what?" said the guide.

She tried to imitate some of the noises. He said something in Spanish, which she didn't get, then he shook his head; he wasn't sure how to explain it in English. Instead he made his hands wide and spread his arms like he was about to conduct an orchestra only he could see, and then he said, "Life." She nodded, and he turned back to his bicycle where already some tourists were climbing into the cart to return to the entrance.

Across the way, she saw the boy and the father walking toward them. Without the breeze created by the movement of the bicycle, she felt the damp heat in a new trickle of sweat that started under her bra.

"Now give it back," said the boy.

The father didn't answer.

"You promised," said the boy, following him. "Mom, tell him to give me the bottle."

She looked at the father, and he said, "I took it away because I thought he'd crack his teeth trying to make those noises in the cart."

"I would've done the same," said the mother to the boy.

"Why do you have to say that?" said the father. "Shouldn't my authority be enough?"

"Of course it is," said the mother.

"He said he'd give it back," said the boy.

"Let's recycle it," said the father. "I'm sure there's a place."

"No, nononono," said the boy.

The mother whispered to the father. "If you said he could have it, you have to give it back. You have to keep your word."

"I'm biting my tongue right now," he whispered back. "So I don't let my word escape." She felt the anger in the very calmness of his voice.

He handed the bottle to the boy, who immediately started blowing on the opening again.

"I'm going to shoot myself," said the father into the mother's ear. "Are you carrying it up the pyramid? All one hundred and twenty steps?" he said aloud to the boy.

The mother imagined the bottle dropping from the boy's hands and clunking down the stone steps, braining an unsuspecting woman from Minnesota. Where would you get an ambulance out here? "Let's put the bottle in a safe place so it doesn't break," said the mother. "I'll stick it in my bag."

"I can't believe we're even talking about this," said the father.

"My poor Coke bottle; I saved your life," said the boy.

That was when the mother realized the girl was no longer with them. "Oh my god," she said.

The father understood right away. "I'm sure she's nearby," he said.

Fecund vegetation grew over everything, as if unchecked since Mayan times. The few directional signs were obscured by foliage and thick, twisting vines. It was impossible to see more than a few yards in each direction. The path in front of them forked two ways.

"This is just what I wanted to do today," the father said, "lose a kid in the largest jungle ruin in Mexico." He went away down one of the paths.

The mother grabbed the boy's wrist—"Ouch!"—"Help me find your sister. You're good at finding things." They speed-walked down the opposite path, which wound through the woods past narrow, unofficial-looking offshoots. She could only hope that her daughter would stay on the main trail. Still, she stopped at each secondary trail and attempted to peer down it, to the place where it disappeared into foliage. "Do you see anything?" she said.

"Look," said the boy. "Ants. Leaf-cutter ants."

"Neato," said the mother, panicked.

Finally, they came into a large clearing. There was the pyramid, towering above them, swarming with tourists.

"I can still see the line of ants," said the boy, pointing to the ground. "Look."

"Do you see your sister?" She stood on tiptoe, as if that would help her get a better view of all the people climbing one hundred feet above her.

"I'll call her," said the boy. "Woorrrt!"

"Please stop that. Mommy's not in the mood."

"Okay," he said, but then worted once more, quietly, for good measure.

Most of the tourists appeared to be with the same group, wearing matching orange visors with black logos. She took the boy by the arm again and dragged him in and out and around the clusters of people. She didn't see her daughter. What was she wearing? You were always supposed to remember what your child was wearing. She saw, instead, her husband.

"Good news," he said. "Both paths lead here. She has to be here."

Unassailable logic. Because there was no way she could have gone back in the other direction, where they'd come from. No she wouldn't have done that, because the signs pointed in this direction, and the main pyramid, the main temple area was this way. She would have been looking for the pyramid. This was a girl who after all could be trusted to kayak safely, staying within view of their house. She wouldn't have gone off down the smaller paths, and if she had, she would have realized her mistake and turned back. That is, if she went under her own power. If she wasn't kidnapped, unremarked by any in this milling crowd as she was grabbed from behind, dragged deep into the woods where there was no path and no busload of tourists and no guides on bikes and no parents and no help and no escape and where her screams—if in fact the hand over her mouth slipped off for even a second, if she thought to bite him and got the sound out before he clamped down harder this time—where her screams would blend with the sounds of the jungle, because now the mother thought of it as the jungle whereas she hadn't before.

As if to reinforce the mother's worst fears, there was a loud high-pitched shriek, heard even above the animated chatter of the sightseers, some of whom stopped to look in the direction of the sound.

"There she is!" said the boy, and there she was, their daughter, at the top of the pyramid, waving frantically and shouting, "Look, Dad! Look, Mom! Come on. Come on."

People on the steps stopped climbing to look at her blonde ponytail bobbing, at her skinny body, her pink Hello Kitty T-shirt stretched over an invisible and unnecessary white training bra and purple shorts. That's what she was wearing.

"That's a relief," said the father.

"Let's climb up and meet your sister at the top," said the mother. But she didn't make a move to the steps. There were a lot of them, and each step was steep but shallow front to back, worn and soft at the edges, as if the pyramid had been made for children. Or by children—lumpy and uneven like an early attempt at sculpting clay. There was a rope running up the center of the stairs for people to hang onto because the steps became progressively steeper the closer you got to the top. It didn't look all that safe. In the States, climbing such a thing might not be allowed. Other countries were always less concerned about safety. Her husband said this was because Americans were more likely to sue.

She hadn't noticed the racing of her heart. What made her think up such awful scenarios? Was it a superstition, that imagining every possible contingency meant none of those things would happen?

"I want to look from here," said the boy. "El Castillo is one hundred thirty-eight feet high."

"Where did you hear that?" said the mother. She looked up at the top, judging. The girl was walking across the upper platform like it was a balance beam. The mother really wanted her to stop that. High places too often reminded her of Donna. She couldn't help imagining it all again, Donna climbing over the rail, Donna jumping off, Donna gone before anyone even knew they should worry about that.

Her husband was on the ground, waving to their daughter, impervious to any apparent danger. Would he be able to protect her? She wanted to ask him, to tell him. She made herself look away. She made herself look at her son.

"It's in the guide book," the boy said.

"Are you sure I can't interest you?" said the father, coming closer to the boy, leaning over, putting a hand on his shoulder.

He ignored the question. "The people on the steps look like beetles."

"You mean ants?" said the mother.

"No, beetles."

The mother watched the adults whose feet were too large for the steps put one hand on a step above, the other on the rope and raise one foot at a time. She had to admit that an awkward beetle was a good approximation.

"You could look from here and then go up. Then you'd get two different views," said the father.

"I'll think about it," said the boy, standing close to his mother but not taking her hand.

"You go ahead," she said. "We'll join you soon."

The father stood for a long moment as if he planned to say something, as if he were keeping himself from saying it. Then he started up the steps.

What was he reining in all the time? She had an imaginary dialogue with him where she asked him couldn't he be patient with their son? Couldn't he stop being angry with her about it? Couldn't he see the boy needed a little something extra from them? Why was he always at odds with a seven-year-old?

She watched him place his feet sideways as he climbed. He was nimble, unlike the beetles. Way up the top, her daughter now sat, waiting, swinging her feet over the edge.

"How about we stand on the bottom step?" said the mother. Because she really did want him to try. She wanted him to come out of whatever it was that was holding him back. She wished she knew what it was.

"No," said the boy.

So she stood there with him and watched. Sweat ran down the middle of her back. The hot dust settled on her skin and stuck there. If she stood long enough, maybe she'd be completely covered in dust. They'd have to unearth her, like the rest of the ruins, and try to figure out her purpose.

"Would you like to see the ball court?"

The voice startled both of them. This guide wasn't the same man who brought them in the cart, but he was wearing the official vest, with a name tag that said "Manuel."

She felt the boy's hand loosen in hers, though she hadn't noticed when he took it.

"What ball game?" she said.

"The ball courts, Mom," said the boy. "The Mayans always had ball courts."

"In the guide book?" she said.

He nodded.

"Mayan football," said the guide. "Have you seen the court?" Manuel spoke better English than the first bicycle guide. He had a heavy accent. It reminded her of Ricardo Montalban. The mother was embarrassed to find that she remembered almost nothing of her Spanish. Had she become one of those people?

"We haven't made it there yet."

"I'll take you, then. It's along the road behind El Castillo."

"How far?" she said.

"Not far, but I suggest you to ride." He indicated his bicycle cart.

"Let's ride in the cart," said the boy.

You want *to go?* the mother had almost asked. "Okay, let's," she said.

Her husband was two-thirds of the way up the pyramid. He was hardly touching the rope. Her daughter clapped her hands and chanted encouragement that the mother couldn't hear.

"Do you know what happened at the ball courts?" Manuel said.

"They played a game like soccer," said the boy. "Except—"

"That is right," said the guide. "Do you like soccer? Which here we call football. Do you play soccer where you live in *los Estados Unidos?*" He looked at the mother when he said this, smiling as if to say he knew the right questions to ask American children. Two of his front teeth were silver.

"No," said the boy. He used to play on a team. The mother had been as glad when he stopped playing as he was. It was difficult to watch him stand in the field, making token efforts to chase after the ball, when he preferred to sit on the sidelines and pull up wide blades of grass to use for whistles.

"Mayan soccer is different," said Manuel, smiling without showing his teeth this time.

"I know," said the boy.

"He read about it," the mother said.

"Do you know what is different?" said the guide, ignoring her.

"The winner gets killed," said the boy.

"You are correct. The winner is sacrificed," said Manuel, not as happily, since he probably liked to explain that part and see the looks on their faces.

"Why would anyone want to win if they're going to get killed?" said the boy.

"Losing is far worse," said Manuel. "Losing is always worse. Winning is honorable. The winner is like a god."

"What happened to the losers?" the boy said.

The mother squinted up at the pyramid to check her husband's progress.

"Come, I'll take you. There you will find a card on the wall that explains all of the rules," said Manuel.

"Look!" She pointed so the boy would see that his father was now at the top. He held their daughter's hand, their hands raised in the air. Gods atop the highest peak.

Manuel held out his hand and helped her climb into the cart. "It's not far," he said again.

"At least if you won, you didn't have to play again," said the boy.

At the ball court, which wasn't far but was farther than she'd hoped, Manuel was in his element. He explained the game and showed them where the players would have been standing. "No hands, only elbows and knees," he said. He demonstrated how the leader served the ball and waited for the boy to try it, to toss out an air ball, which (to her surprise) he did without hesitation. Then he had the boy stand where another teammate would stand and showed him how to field the invisible ball. Again, the boy tried it himself, and Manuel congratulated him. It was like having a private soccer coach. There was even, at one point, a high five.

Manuel led them to a carving in the stone wall on one side of the court. "Now to see this: a jaguar, a very important animal to Mayans and to Mexico. Here it is having its head cut off. And there, a player has his heart cut out." He said this with matter-of-fact sternness. "Sometimes the winner wasn't sacrificed; sometimes it was the losing side in a war. Then, it is not an honor. The outcome is set before the start. The team that is assigned to lose must lose, and then they are killed. Those were the rituals that archaeologists understand to happen."

The boy stared at the carved jaguar.

"Your turn," Manuel said to the mother. "Stand here. You are the captain, and he is a player. Show how you serve the ball."

She wanted to set a good example. She swung her arms the way she thought she'd seen him do it.

"No, Miss, try it again. Like so."

She did it again. Manuel cocked his head in a gesture that seemed to mean "so-so."

Now it was a challenge. She would show him. She was anything but so-so in her day, when she played field hockey—not soccer, because no one played soccer then. She wasn't a star, but they could count on her. She loved the feeling of competence when she picked off a pass, when she evaded the girls who were bigger and stronger than she was. She'd almost forgotten how good she was and how many bruises there were on her shins, black and blue points of pride, despite or even because of the shin guards they wore; they were stiff and hard as bones.

Now Manuel came behind her, close. He wouldn't try anything, would he? There was the boy, watching. A ridiculous thought; it seemed like forever since anyone—She swung her arm back, bent at the elbow. Manuel grabbed her forearm and held it.

"You can do it, Mom," the boy said. "It's not that hard."

"Here is what you did," said Manuel. He moved her arm forward and back again. "Now here is what you are supposed to do. Not so stiff. Relax. That's better." And he swung her arm back again, and it did feel different, more power behind it.

"Very much better," he said. "Loosen your shoulders." He rested his hands on her shoulders and jiggled them a little.

"Again," said Manuel, keeping his hand on her arm as she brought it back.

She had been brave back then. She'd taken a stick to the skull. A concussion ended her season, and her parents took her out of the sport altogether. Not a sport for an intelligent girl, they said. Need to protect your brains first, they said.

All of a sudden, she was angry.

She threw out the imaginary ball, and the boy pretended to field it with his knee and then bounce it off of his elbow.

"*Muy bueno!*" Manuel said.

"Do I win or lose?" said the boy.

"In fact, you lose to play another day," said Manuel. "But someday it will be your turn to win." He smiled with silver, and winked.

"And then . . ." The boy drew his index finger across his neck, a slashing motion.

"Don't lose your head," said Manuel. A colloquialism he could only have picked up from the tourists. His hand returned to the mother's shoulder, rested gently near a wisp of hair that had escaped from where she'd piled it under her sunhat. She felt it tickle her neck. Or was that his thumb?

"We should go back," she said. "My husband will be looking for us." But in the tiniest way, she didn't want to go back. She wanted to stay with this strange man's hand on her shoulder a little longer, to feel its ordinary kindliness, its undemanding, even indifferent, affection.

"You have a good arm," said Manuel, which he now rubbed, his hand traveling over her flabby triceps. "You can practice"—and here he stopped and searched for the word—"technique." She might have only imagined how boldly he looked at her face just then, when he said, "Your husband would be happy to learn this game, too, yes?"

"Thank you," she said. "I wish we had time. It's a long drive back." She wished Manuel hadn't reminded her of her existence outside of this ruin. That other ruin, she thought.

"Your son knows how to do. The boy can teach him!"

She was so at sea in this exchange, she couldn't be sure what was real and what she'd only layered with extra meaning in her imagination.

"*Pero*," Manuel went on, "you should not teach him. Men don't like to learn such games from their wives." He didn't smile. She didn't need to remember her schooling to understand what he meant by that.

After Manuel drove them back to where he found them, she gave him a large tip, larger than she gave the man who drove them all the way to the center of the complex. Manuel's smile in response was perfunctory and polite, no display of metal.

"That is your husband," he said, as he helped the boy out of the cart. "In the blue shirt?"

She turned and saw him. That was her husband.

"You should have seen the way down, Mom! It was awesome." The girl ran to her and grabbed her arms, pulling them down when she said "down" and then up to show how high. "It was straight down."

"That sounds thrilling," the mother said.

"It was like hanging from a rope in the sky attached to an airplane," said her daughter. "I wish you had come."

"I will next time," she said. She hoped there would be another chance. This couldn't be the only chance. She was feeling angry again. She glanced around for a stone to kick. She was angry at herself. Why didn't she do something? If she wanted anything to change, she was going to have to be the one to start. So why couldn't she act?

She might get bruised, and she wasn't used to it anymore.

"You can't hang from a rope attached to an airplane," said the boy. "Only from a helicopter. Airplanes can't hover." He reached into the mother's bag and extracted his Coke bottle.

"Oh whatever. Does he have to ruin everything?" said the girl.

"I learned to play Mayan football," said the boy. "And you didn't."

"You were great at Mayan football," said the mother, "but you don't have to—"

"Good. Maybe they'll sacrifice you," said the girl.

"*Worrrt*," went the boy.

"Stop it. Will you stop it?" said the father.

The mother looked around and noticed Manuel, or the bicycle she thought was his, departing with another pair of tourists in the cart.

➔

On the patio, she gathered the empty beer bottles that were left out-side the night before. Inside, the husband was in charge of bedtime rituals. There was shouting. She heard the boy through the closed door. She wondered if their landlord would hear. She walked away to the water until she couldn't hear even the tinny echo of their shouts. The waves quite literally drowned them out. She sat down in the sand and picked up a shell that turned out to be a hermit crab. She watched its legs go.

The patio door opened and the shouts spilled out into the night. The boy was running toward her, crying. He opened his fist; inside was a handful of glass.

SELF REPORT

SHE WASN'T SURPRISED to end up in his office, but she'd always thought it would be about her son, not her daughter. There was a lesson in it: instead of worrying about the ones who didn't fit in, you should worry about the ones who seemed to fit in too well.

"It's not uncommon," he said, clasping his hands together at his chin and watching her intently as if her nonverbal response was as important as anything she might say.

"You mean it's common?" she said.

"What we want to know," he said, "is what's behind it."

Considering the wait to see him—six agonizing weeks—and the price—like admission to a private club, especially if you added in the sense of privilege that came from getting a slot on his calendar, she'd expected nicer furnishings. The sagging, threadbare loveseat she was sitting on reminded her of the one in her parents' house, before they'd slipcovered it.

"A boy with a camera. That's what was behind it," she said.

He wrote something on a pad: *The mother guards with sarcasm,* she guessed.

She fiddled with the cup he'd given her. There was a ring left inside it from some past cup of coffee. The way to avoid that was a dark-colored mug. Maybe he had a suggestion box. Had she been drinking from a cup last used by an unstable person? But no; he was an adolescent psychologist. The parents were the ones who sat here holding this cup as if waiting for someone to walk by and stuff a dollar in.

"Would you say your daughter's behavior in this instance was unusual?" he said. "Has she taken unusual risks in the past?"

"Is she a risk-taker?" the mother said.

"Let's not use a label," he said.

He was progressive, of course. That's what people said about him. And if you hadn't heard, you'd see it right away. His hair was long, first of all. Long and gray and wavy, pulled back in a ponytail. He wore a wrinkled blue button-down and faded khakis and small, round John Lennon glasses. There was a guitar propped in the corner. When he wasn't writing on his pad, he sat with his chin on his folded hands, or spread his legs apart, his elbows resting on his knees, and dangled his clasped hands in front of his crotch.

What would constitute an unusual risk? A six-year-old, say, who likes to go down the slide head first, even after the first set of stitches? A ten-year-old who climbs inside a storm pipe to go after a ball, despite being told of the danger? An eleven-year-old who wanders off during a vacation in Rome? A thirteen-year-old who takes a ride home from school even though she can't name the person who drove her? Were these normal risks for a child? Because you see the mother's only basis for comparison was the boy who was the opposite of risk-taking. Or maybe he took intellectual risks, while his sister took physical ones. But shouldn't a child be a little bit afraid?

"No," said the mother. "Nothing that seemed unusual at the time."

"There's a scale I use to measure impulsivity," he said. "You filled out the questionnaire. I'll have your daughter take a test that's a good indicator of speedy decision-making."

Speedy? "That's bad, right?"

"What we hope to see is an indication of decision-making that can be compared favorably with her age group."

"Meaning?"

"Does she take a moment to think something through before she acts," he said. "There are people who think things through and still make what we generally consider the wrong decision. That's one kind of problem. Then there are those whose brains don't permit them the time to make the right decision; they may even realize it after, when it's too late. They've acted, essentially, without thinking. Teens are already challenged in that area. That's normal brain development. But, some teens are more challenged than average, and then we see trouble." He stopped talking and shuffled through a folder.

Trouble, with a capital T, and that rhymes with We. At a loss, she searched for a place to put down her empty mug. There were stacks of books or papers on every surface, but there was a smidge of space within reach, on an end table next to a pile of manila folders. When she leaned over to put the cup down, she could read the names on the tabs. All five of them were boys. How could he leave them sitting out like that? What if she knew those boys? Worse yet, what if her daughter knew those boys? She memorized the names.

"You and your husband are together?" he said.

He was looking at the forms she'd filled out. "Yes," she said. She'd checked that box, despite how easy it would have been to check a different one. Want a quick separation? Just check the box.

She had horrible thoughts. Her resentment was unfair, she told herself again. Her husband wasn't sitting here in this office with her because he was in his office making the money to pay for this visit to Dr. G, even though he didn't quite agree with its necessity and whatever she ended up telling him about it before or after the fact would lead to an argument. Didn't agree at all. Had called it "a family matter, a matter of discipline, not a mental disorder." As if she, the mother, wanted it to be a mental disorder. But if this was a part of normal adolescent development, why weren't all the girls letting boys take photos of their naked body parts?

"And you present a united front, consistent with rules and discipline?" said Dr. G.

She sensed a trap. Do any parents present a united front? That was just something they told you to do in those T. Berry Brazelton books. Maybe old T. Berry could spend the day at her house and unite things a little.

"What are you getting at?" she said. "Are you saying this is our fault? For not being strict enough?" Dr. G was waving his hand as if asking for a turn to correct her impression. A gray curl came loose and fell over his eye. But she kept going. "Because you don't have to. I know it's my fault."

He smiled at her then. He had a way of grinning, slightly open-mouthed, so you could see his top teeth, which were nice and straight. He had smiled in this same way when he shook her hand and told her to call him Greg. His last name was difficult to pronounce. She had taught it to herself incorrectly and had to unlearn it once his receptionist said it to her the right way, when she'd called for the appointment. She could say it now; she'd had six weeks to prepare. But no, he wouldn't hear of her calling him anything other than Greg, which was a short version of his last name. She thought of him as Dr. G. When he first gave her the smile, she was left wondering what he'd decided not to say, until she saw him do it more than once and realized nothing else was hiding behind it.

She was in a constant state of reorientation. She had thought that time and experience made one's impressions more accurate, but in fact what age and experience had taught her was that there were no reliable impressions. People were situational, inconsistent, compartmentalized, proud and ashamed. The best you could do was to decide what you could live with and what you could live without, make your bed and get to the business of lying in it. Not resignation, not acceptance, not making the best of it, but trying to enjoy it every now and then. That was what she'd decided. That was what she'd been preparing to implement: allowing the phoenix satisfaction to rise from the ashes of her dissatisfaction. It was a goal.

And then the photos had happened. She'd wanted to shake her daughter when she found out, shake her until all those disconnected pieces of her brain that Dr. G had mentioned landed in the right position. She was fourteen, yes, but looked twenty. Her body did, as if she'd switched places with someone overnight and ended up inside a Hooters waitress.

They say the oxygen mask will drop down automatically. They tell you the seatback cushion doubles as a flotation device. But when she imagined her daughter's breasts displayed on smartphones and iPads and sexy screensavers, passed around like baseball cards— "I'll trade you Rachel's tits for Rebecca's ass"—she felt she might be drowning, and all the rescue apparatuses failed to activate. One of these photographs had found its way onto the Internet. Her headless daughter, divvied up. It was as if someone had flown overhead in an airplane, scattering pictures of her child's body over seven continents. Were people staring at her daughter's muff in South Africa? Were her breasts big in Russia? She sounded cavalier even to herself, when she was anything but. Anything. Her daughter had not quite understood, or had not allowed herself to understand, that these photos could never be recalled from circulation. It would be like collecting scattered nuclear waste.

Dr. G was talking about cognitive skills testing, stimulation-seeking measures, processing challenges, scales and inventories. A vast inventory of inventories, this man had. Which reminded her of the string of bad retail jobs she'd held while she was in school. The dreaded inventory days, every last item recorded and accounted for. The sheer drudgery might have been what kept her in school, the threat of a lifetime of inventory days. And now, here it was, they were going to take an inventory of her daughter. Would they record each hangnail? Each false assumption? Errant fantasy? If she submitted her daughter for such scrutiny, what of real value would they learn?

As he described the testing process, he put down his pad and walked over to his desk to pick up the phone receiver. It was an old corded phone. He took off his glasses and pressed some buttons, tapped a Morse code with the hang-up button, and listened, presumably for a dial tone. "Excuse me," he said. "Technical problem." And then, into the phone, "No just trying to . . ." He pressed the hang-up button again and put down the receiver.

Dr. G's office was a time warp. Here she was discussing an incident that could not have occurred back when that phone was first installed at that desk. And she was doing so while seated on a sofa exactly like the one her parents had owned, the one where she and Jonathan Hartman held their weekly make-out sessions her senior year of high school. Jonathan Hartman, whom she'd secretly nicknamed the Magic Finger.

"When we were that age—" Dr. G was saying.

Was he saying she was that age at the same time he was? She doubted it. He was at least fifteen years older. She'd examined his diplomas on the wall while she waited.

Her parents' loveseat was green, a velvety finish but with most of the nap rubbed off and even more distressed than Dr. G's, so that when she and Jonathan were in the throes one night, when he pressed her into the cushion, the foam rubber bits escaped from a place where the fabric was worn through and scattered themselves throughout her hair. She was still finding them the next morning, like a trail of breadcrumbs leading her back to where she started, to the moment right before Jonathan Hartman showed her that he knew what no other boy had yet been able to successfully demonstrate—exactly where to put his fingers and how to manipulate them for best results.

She could not even think what she might have done, at "that age," if she or Jonathan had had not only a camera but a means of mass distribution. You couldn't take that kind of film to the Fotomat. They would have told your parents. The biggest threat to her privacy had been the Polaroid camera. Somewhere in her history there was an ill-considered Polaroid picture. At least one. And she supposed it was possible, now that there were scanners, to put such a photograph online.

"—the consequences," he went on, "were a different kind of dire. You had to deal with your mistakes, but you didn't have to deal with your mistakes becoming so readily and irretrievably public."

There was a beep, and they both started. The beeping continued in a steady rhythm, like a heart monitor. It was the phone. Dr. G grabbed for the receiver and pressed buttons. The beeping stopped.

"It's a lot to expect," he said, shaking his head. "To navigate these new waters. Takes more self-control than most. Than most kids can muster." He came back and sat in the chair facing her, took his glasses off and put them on again. As he talked, he molded a globe in the air with his hands.

She'd had to give up Jonathan Hartman's magic finger. To let it go. (She amused herself. It was all she had that was her own—her private amusement, held up in the face of circumstances that defied her with their undeniable seriousness.) Her relationship with Jonathan became impossible to sustain because the more he saw of her, the more he also saw of her parents, and while his finger had its remarkable insights, Jonathan's insight into the rest of what made her tick seemed less remarkable. He'd come over each week and chat up her parents for upwards of thirty minutes. Each time it took longer to get out of the house. Jonathan had gone beyond the simple requirement to kiss up prior to feeling up and had taken a genuine liking to her parents.

She remembered waiting, sour, sullen, in an armchair, pointedly not the loveseat, shaking her leg to give herself the illusion of being on the move. Didn't he notice how badly she wanted to get out of there? She sent him mental signals: *Hello? Jonathan?*

She didn't tell him anything. She didn't say that she didn't want to go out with him anymore. She just stopped returning his calls.

THERE WAS A tapping at the door. Dr. G opened it a crack. The mother smelled sandalwood, like the incense she used to burn to cover up other smells. She heard the receptionist say she was going to get some lunch and could she bring him anything. The woman craned her neck and peered around him, gave the mother a nod of recognition and the mother smiled. No, no, he told her. He seemed to body-block the doorway to keep the receptionist from entering the room.

He closed the door, took a breath, put his hands on his hips and considered his shoes, which were scuffed. "You can start filling out these reports. You'll see the scale. I'll have your daughter complete self-reports with similar categories." He didn't move, kept examining his shoes; then he seemed to remember she was there, looked up, and pulled off his glasses again to search through the stacks on his desk. He dug up some papers but didn't hand them to her.

Her parents had asked her when she would be seeing that nice Jonathan again. She looked at her mother and said with a straight face, "It didn't work out. He wanted to go all the way, and I'm not ready." Shocking with apparent candor had been a specialty of hers. It worked; there were no further questions about Jonathan Hartman.

"My daughter's never been on a date," she said to Dr. G.

"That you know of," he said. "What we used to call a date has evolved. Parents don't always recognize the signs."

What she'd recognized was that one day her daughter was wearing a bra and didn't need one, and the next day she needed one. It had come too easily. The girl didn't appreciate it; she didn't understand what it meant.

ONCE, JONATHAN HAD taken her on a picnic in the park. He packed a lunch for them. A high school boy—can you imagine that? He fixed her lunch. They ate on a blanket in the grass, and then Jonathan sang to her. She remembered the sun making white spots on the grass while she lay on her back near the blanket and drank Coke spiked with rum that Jonathan had taken from his father's stash of airplane miniatures. He sang madrigals in the school choir, but when he sang to her he sang a song that was popular then, a slow song called "I'm Not in Love." At one point, he pulled her up by the arm and she stood and he held her and they slow-danced on the grass to his singing. *I'm not in love, so don't forget it. / It's just a silly phase I'm going through.*

It came back to her in a rush now; she had indeed forgotten it.

It was as if they were alone in the universe, even though there were children playing Frisbee, and families having their own picnics were scattered over the wide field of grass. Voices would occasionally arrive to pierce their solitude, and one of these times, she broke from

Jonathan and took off toward the woods. He followed. She found a packed dirt trail and decided to see where it led. Without any discussion about where they were going or why, they just went. When they could no longer see where they once were and the voices from the park were like far off birds, Jonathan grabbed her and pulled her to the ground with him. They'd left the blanket so they lay half in the undergrowth beside the trail and half directly in the dirt. They kissed, each tasting the same rum, and pressed against each other for as long as they could stand it. Never had her clothing felt so unnatural; she wanted nothing more than to take it all off and be naked with him in the woods. She felt intensely that she loved him and that he was a part of her, though she'd never fucked him and, as it turned out, never would, yet she felt him inside her. His face was hot on her neck, and they were breathing like one person.

It may have been the most perfect time she ever had with a boy. The sun was coming through the dense canopy, having moved while they were underneath it, and her shirt was off and so was his, and they just lay there together, holding onto each other, as if one of them would be leaving forever as soon as they let go.

It was weeks, maybe only days after that that she stopped returning Jonathan's calls. And by the next day, he had poison ivy.

She'd been dazzled not only by the sun, but by what was possible, by the mystery of all that lay ahead of her. To set one piece of the puzzle in place, an immovable piece—to make Jonathan that piece—would mean that the other pieces must fit in around him. What if they didn't?

Jonathan was the last person who sang to her. The last who sang and meant it.

DR. G WAS BLURRY. Her eyes were filled, God damn it—the older she got the easier it was to cry, so easy that half the time she didn't

174

know she was doing it. He handed her a box of tissues. She dismissed the offer with a wave, but then took the box anyway, took a tissue, and held onto it. Dr. G looked like he was underwater. He dragged his chair closer and leaned in, as if they might otherwise be overheard. She had an urge to remove her shoes and pull her feet up under herself on the couch to make herself into a tight ball, to hold herself until she became calm again. She didn't do it. She uncrossed and recrossed her legs, realized she had torn the unused tissue to shreds in her hand.

"This is a lot to manage," Dr. G said. He stroked his fingers and looked at them as if they were giving him pain.

"I'm sorry," she said. "I'm here about my daughter. I'm embarrassed. This," she indicated her damp face, "is ridiculous."

She took another tissue and this time wiped her eyes. Then she did what she'd been thinking of, pulled her legs up under herself and hid her face in the crook of her arm.

"It's okay to feel it," said Dr. G.

Normally that kind of remark would make her want to snipe back a sarcastic barb. But things were not normal, and when was the last time they had been?

"You're human," said the doctor. He put a hand on her shoulder. "It can't be helped." He sighed. He came and sat next to her on the couch.

She opened her eyes. His face was close.

"You're very pretty," he said. He let his hand slip across her back so that his arm was around her. She didn't pull away, and he held her, her face in his shoulder, tucked in the hollow below his collarbone. She felt his chest rise and fall with breathing and felt the steady rhythm of his heart as if it was reaching for her, trying to reach her. It didn't seem wrong.

JUST SEX

"THIS EVER HAPPEN to you?" said Pogo.

I answered honestly, "No," and then thought I should have lied and said "yes" to spare his feelings. "All the time!" I could have said. "It's not you, it's me," I could have said. "I'm a buzz-killer."

This was a mellower Pogo than the one I recalled as always ready, willing, and able, even after a half-dozen cocktails. But there were remnants of his old theatricality, his ringmaster persona. The first thing he said to me when I walked in was, "Let me look at you, Miranda Weber." He'd spun me around and sniffed every inch of me and declared that I looked better now. That was his idea of a compliment.

Why had I agreed to meet him? Not for revenge, because, if revenge was my goal, half-naked wasn't the way to get there, unless I was a gladiator.

"Not a drink, either," he said, meaning he'd had nothing to drink, which I'd noticed. He told me, before we took half our clothes off, that he'd stopped.

"It doesn't matter," I said. "Don't worry about it."

"Look at that," he said, and smacked me on my naked bottom so it stung and then slapped at his dick like it was one of the Three Stooges. The bald one. "What the fuck is wrong with you?" He was talking to it now.

"Do you want me to go?" I said and then realized I'd made it worse, as if there was no reason for me to be there if he wasn't going to perform. Then again, *was* there another reason?

"No," he said. "Stay here, Weber." He sounded preoccupied, but he put his hand on my ass again, this time gently stroking.

Maybe he didn't mean it, but I wanted to stay, so I did.

IT WASN'T ONE of those things where I could have said later, "It just happened." As if we were working overtime together, went for a drink after, found ourselves pulled by a Jedi-like force, and suddenly we were naked behind the horizontal files among the missing paper clips, carpet burns on my ass, no.

"This is a nice hotel," I'd said when I got there. "I've never been in a room here before."

"Why are you talking so much?" he said, and covered my mouth with his hand and pushed me back on the bed.

WHEN A MAN says, "Come to my hotel," it generally means one thing.

Despite that, I wasn't sure what to expect when I got his email. I wasn't sure what he was really asking of me. So I'd asked, "Do you want to have lunch?" and he'd replied, "If our appetites turn to food."

He gave me his room number. I walked through the hotel lobby like a guest, past the mahogany desk and the potted palms and the boutique. I went straight up in the elevator, thinking, "I've never done this before. I'm going to a man's hotel room." I murmured it, as if I was talking dirty to myself, all along the carpeted hall—"man's hotel room; man's hotel room"—noting as I went that even in nice hotels the carpet was bad. The pattern was always loud. It made me feel like something was shouting at me, but its voice was muffled by my footsteps.

"Shut up, carpet. I'm going to a man's hotel room," I said. "Don't say a word." Someone else came out of a room, walked past me in the other direction and looked at me as if I was out of place.

It hadn't occurred to me to worry that someone might see me coming or going, that I might need an explanation for what I was doing on the tenth floor of the Shoreham in the middle of the day. And wasn't it just like Pogo to choose a place like that? The shabby genteel luxury.

"I belong here," I thought. "I belong wherever I decide to go." Or maybe I'd spoken it aloud to the carpet. Maybe that's why the woman stared. And that's when I understood that I was angry, but for what and at whom? Because of time passing? I did sometimes want to pull it back, like a curtain, but it got away from me, instead like a rope in tug of war. I hadn't seen Pogo in more than twenty-five years.

I don't know if I should have been surprised how easily I fell back in with him. It was like olfactory memory, there we were again, brought back to a place where we knew just what to do to each other. It was a relief. Or it could be. Except that by some fluke, he couldn't, and we hadn't, yet.

What was I prepared to overlook? What excuses would I make to myself? I already associated Pogo with what might have been the first irredeemable act of my life. And if it was my irredeemable act, it was his, too. When you ended a pregnancy that was never supposed to have happened in the first place, was that what people called "unfinished business"?

179

BEFORE I WENT to meet Pogo that first time, I was drinking my morning coffee, blinking out the window like I always did. I saw the red-tailed hawk again, the one I'd been watching for a week. It was perched in the same spot on the neighbor's rusty swing set. I looked through binoculars to be sure, the same binoculars I took to concerts so that I could watch the beads of sweat roll down the back of the conductor's neck and into his collar. The swing set wasn't the highest point by any stretch. There were all those oak trees. But the bird liked it there. I could see the strong hooked beak, the large claws scratching at the peeled paint. The bird's chest was speckled; it was a juvenile. It's not that I knew birds so well, but I knew which ones passed through my yard, from years of watching. Once, there was a pair of mallards, obviously lost, hoping for a pond and finding only the standing water on the patio, where the mosquitoes gathered on humid days. The ducks flew off. There were multitudes of city birds—sparrows of all types that I couldn't identify, plus woodpeckers, tiny chickadees, grackles that sounded like my cousin's kid learning the Suzuki method, robins of course, and cardinals, and nasty nest-invading blue jays.

For work, I wrote short articles ostensibly about those birds, and other wildly random topics, for websites focused on gardening and landscape, or home décor, or for dubious parenting websites, all sponsored by drug companies or fertilizer companies or pest control or real estate concerns. I was called a "content provider."

The job I had before that, as a marketing strategist, disappeared in the recession. But once, some years back, Pogo's company had hired my company to spread sunshine about them. So I'd heard about him and even received occasional formal work-related email updates that went to vast numbers of recipients, but I'd never heard from him directly, not until now.

I admit to some morbid curiosity, because who didn't want to know what direction your life might have taken had you followed that other path? Even so, I'd never thought to contact him. And then things changed.

THREE WEEKS BEFORE Pogo sent me an email asking me to meet him, I sat across the desk from Dr. Nina, my gynecologist, and stared at a pamphlet she'd passed to me, face down, like a dirty secret. On the cover was a photo of a smiling woman wearing a cornflower-blue sweater-set and neat denim jeans. Her thick gray hair was styled to appear effortless and natural. She was one of those women who looks fabulous with gray hair, which I never would. A bicycle was parked behind her. There was a blue sky. The title on the pamphlet read, "The Change and You."

"Perimenopause," Dr. Nina had said. And my blood tests indicated the rest of it, without the qualifier, would happen sooner rather than later. She had, in the past, warned of pending hormonal "transitions," but I'd thought of it all as far off in the future, a time when I wouldn't mind wearing stretch-waist pants and Hush Puppies and eating dinner at four o'clock. Not now, now was too soon; I wasn't even fifty, not for a few more months. Weren't you supposed to be at least fifty when your body dried up from the inside leaving only a husk?

On the wall behind Nina's desk was an autographed publicity still from the movie *Thelma and Louise*, a framed photo of the two actresses, Susan Sarandon and Geena Davis, in the front seat of a convertible. I'd stared at that photo plenty of times in the past, but never saw it quite as I did now. It was the scene just before they drove off the cliff. I wanted to climb into the back seat and sail off with them. I slumped in Nina's tastefully upholstered guest chair—a busy but muted pattern that wouldn't show stains, convenient for crying on. Or vomiting. I thought I might do both.

"Nina," I finally said, "I'm losing my mind."

I WOKE UP one morning having transformed into a cockroach. One day I was my normal, within-bounds horny self, the horny self I'd lived with for decades, the one that fantasized over the good parts in *A Sport and a Pastime* and watched Paul Newman in *Hud* over and over. In what seemed like no more than a day, I'd revved into a freakish sexual overdrive. I couldn't look at a cucumber without getting excited. I could come just daydreaming about coming. I never knew when my brain would be flooded with longing. And I didn't want it to end.

I tried Internet porn. But most of it was no sexier than my grandmother's third husband's dick, which I'd seen when I was seven and made me laugh even then. The women with big hair and press-on nails annoyed me; their orgasms were as fake as their manicures. I wanted to see actual enjoyment. I wanted to be convinced. False ecstasy was coupled with the too-real—the viscous fluids in volumes suitable for drowning, the close-up angles on dank orifices. And all of them shaved like patients prepped for surgery. I felt not like a voyeur but like a doctor diagnosing the clinical manifestations of pleasure.

I still got off. Because I got off no matter what. But in the end, watching wasn't enough. I wanted to touch someone real, besides myself.

DR. NINA UNDERSTOOD when to be silently dismissive, when nonsense was nonsense, when I was only talking to myself, and when I was bargaining. Imagine how differently a psychotherapy session would go if you had to do the first half with your feet in the stirrups and the second half sitting in a chair, feeling like K-Y Jelly was leaking into your underwear.

I told Nina how often I was masturbating. She didn't blink.

"That will go away when the hormone levels decrease," she said. "Your body's preparing to stop manufacturing estrogen. You're experiencing a hormonal imbalance in the range of normal for this process."

"I don't want it to go away," I said. "It's like being reincarnated. As, I don't know, Dona Juana."

"It will," she said, handing me an order for a mammogram and a DEXA scan.

"Start taking calcium," Nina said.

THE MORNING I went to meet Pogo for a second time, I watched the hawk out the window again. It had relocated to a new perch on a fence post. It stood perfectly still, almost like those plastic owls people put out to deter rodents. In a moment, the hawk turned its head, following the movements of something I couldn't see. Its sharp eye and the arrangement of its plumage gave it an arched brow, regal and terrible. Was it thinking about anything besides its next meal?

Before I left the house, I wrote a piece about rodents and raptors, which would be linked to ads for a company that manufactured mousetraps. If you didn't have a hawk on your fence, those traps might come in handy.

"I GO BY Porter now," Pogo said. Porter was his real name. "I told you that last month. Did you forget?" I hadn't forgotten. When we were dating, no one was allowed to call him Porter. Now, he told me, only his brother still called him Pogo.

"Okay," I said. "If you're a Porter, will you carry my bags for me?"

"I can't," he said. "I'm overburdened." He put his hand in his pants. "Let me show you."

Even with the act he put on, he seemed subdued. Or somehow conscious of me in a different way than before. I caught him watching me with a funny expression. Was it regret?

"How's Cheever?" I asked. My family never gave people nicknames; you were who you were, and that was that. I'd tried, over the years to establish a nickname for myself, but it never stuck. Dona Juana was sounding better and better.

"Still 'cheeving," said Pogo. "He and Natasha have two kids in college, one out."

"Wow," I said. "They're still married."

"Yes," said Pogo. "I'm Uncle Porter. And a godfather," he said.

He told me he traveled a lot. "Rubbing shoulders with the fat cats," he said. "With the finest people, my dear. Every night, a soiree." He liked to joke, except now his banter had a tired edge, like an aging actor who was always expected to play the same role, the one that once made him famous. He slipped into it easily.

"I have a beach house," he said. He didn't say which beach. Maybe the house was inherited. I remembered how he once went to his parents' beach house when we were dating, and he didn't invite me. He took someone else. Funny how he was trying to impress me now, when back then he seemed to feel that he didn't have to.

"I must look dang old to you," he said. Seeing him again after so long was like artificial aging in the movies, like they'd etched on some wrinkles and powdered his hair. At least he had his hair, though it was shorter. His potbelly was there, but smaller. Most of him seemed smaller. There was a thin scar on his temple that I didn't remember.

"Do I?" I said. "Look old?"

"You're a young, young lady, and I'm a dirty old man," he said.

He told me he was divorced "an arm and a leg ago." I wanted to know more, but I didn't ask. Curiosity, that killer, had brought me so far. Would it get me the rest of the way?

"Your hair's darker," he said. He wound it around his finger and stuck his finger in his mouth.

"I dye it," I said.

He grabbed more of my hair and pulled my head back, exposing my neck, which he kissed.

"I'll be sixty," he said to my Adam's apple.

"I'm jailbait," I said.

He unzipped his pants and slid my underwear to my knees. I still had my blouse on. We thrashed around on the bed until the moment of truth, when the same thing happened as the first time. Now, I was going to blame myself.

"This cock is for the birds," said Pogo, staring at his dick, which was drooping like a wet flag at half-mast.

"Can I . . . do something?" I said.

"No," he said. He got up and filled a glass with ice then opened the minibar and poured a bourbon. "Want some?" he said, after he'd swallowed about half of it.

"Yes," I said. "And no." I was worried about the smell. I put my arms around his neck and kissed him, sweeping up bourbon with my tongue instead.

We were slow and cautious when my pulse was beating in my ears and the last thing I wanted was slow. Pressed up against him and his smell of lime and bourbon, I wanted to shred his clothes and sink into his skin. The rest of it seemed innocent, tentative, almost old fashioned. Even the part where we were naked for each other, with our older imperfect bodies obscured and transfigured by the memories of our younger imperfect ones.

➔

When I got home that night, I weighed my guilt. I didn't count the way I touched him before nothing happened, or the way he touched me. Was I deficient in conscience? All my life I'd felt compelled to take responsibility for things that were impossible for me to control, and now, this thing I could control, it was a choice I could make or not make, yet it seemed disconnected from any moral consequence. The decision was made when I walked into his room and subverted only by anatomical failure.

I put music on and put dinner on the table and poured wine, and Devin came home and kissed me on the mouth and sat down opposite me and said, "You look good tonight, Ms. Weber."

I came back to myself, to my real life, as if my afternoon was only a play I'd acted out in my head. "As do you, Mr. Shields," I said.

"The kids away," said Devin, "agrees with both of us."

It had been just the two of us for about a year, barring college breaks, one of which had just ended. The cliché about not knowing what to do in an empty nest, that wasn't the problem. The problem was that long ago we'd both disappeared into our own lives. When we reached for each other, it was an afterthought in the blind dark. I knew where he'd touch me and for how long: lips and then, briefly, nipples, then a finger inside me, then his cock. I could have set a timer. I tried to shake things up. I read books—new uses for my tongue, undiscovered erogenous zones—but I felt him resisting.

Did he have someone else? I wasn't sure I wanted to know.

Neither of us acknowledged that the emptiness had nothing to do with our kids leaving. We lived by the script.

WHEN PEOPLE GOT back with old lovers, they said things like, "It felt like going home," or "It was as if we never left." It wasn't that way with Pogo. I was half mad as hell at myself and at the same time half liberated, in a way that would have been no different if we were both still single. There'd been other opportunities, and I'd passed. Did I realize that all I'd done was trade one kind of safety for another?

When we were dating, and he could take me or leave me, it mattered too much to me. Now it mattered little. I was there, I told myself, for one thing: just sex. The one thing, probably the only thing, we'd always done well.

WHEN I WAS twenty-two and found out I was pregnant, I'd waited a while to tell Pogo about it. I'd wanted to decide for myself what to do before he had a chance to talk me into or out of something.

"I'm happy for them," I'd said, that day. I was talking about Cheever and Natasha. I was half-lying. This was after they'd told us they were getting married and having a baby, pretty much at the same time.

"It'll last a week," Pogo had said. "Those crazy kids." He used his TV-dad voice.

"They seem excited about it." But I couldn't be sure. Maybe they were acting, too.

"Cheever's kicking me out of the house," said Pogo. "That's why he got her pregnant. He needed an excuse to get rid of me. I guess he won that round."

"I don't think he was playing any round," I said. "I think he's in love."

"Sure, sure," said Pogo, patting me on the arm like I was a dim old lady. "Whatever you say, dearie. Ah, to be young and in love."

"Doesn't it seem like he loves her?"

"*Havin' my baby!*" he sang. "*What a beautiful way to say . . .*"

"Cut it out."

"*. . . that you love me. Havin' my baby—*"

"Shut it." That was the time to tell him. If there was ever going to be a time. He might appreciate the irony. I couldn't get the words out.

"I don't know if I want to see Wesley and Kim today," I said, instead. We were in Georgetown on our way to visit Pogo's friends. Wesley and Kim had had a baby. As if everyone and their baby had to be in my face.

"Come on, Weber," he said. "Turn that frown upside down. It'll be entertaining." He was always saying something that would sound stupid coming from anyone else; when he said it, it still sounded stupid but also funny.

"They're bored out of their minds," said Pogo. "They want visitors."

Wesley and Kim had named their baby "Clementine," as if they couldn't wait to get rid of her. The last time we saw them, Clementine had been barely a month old. And I hadn't been pregnant. I didn't remember noticing her particularly. Before you had your own baby, those belonging to other people were like accessories, as if the parents brought you into their living room and said, "Look, here's our new Turkish carpet; oh and here's our new baby, too."

Last time, I held Clementine. It was considered polite for female guests to hold the baby. And good training. You rarely heard male guests asking for a turn. They were satisfied to put it off until their turn came in the way that was unavoidable.

Pogo and I walked down a steep cobblestone hill, not talking. It was cool out, and I wished I'd worn a sweater. Pogo lit a cigarette. He only smoked when he'd been drinking. I only smoked his cigarettes. He held it out to me, but I didn't take it.

"Suit yourself," he said.

"Stop for a second," I said, stopping. It was late afternoon on a

weekday, and there was no one else around. We'd even found parking. I'd called in sick to work. When I was pregnant, I almost always
felt queasy. I told them I had a stomach bug. "Before we go in," I
said, "there's something I need to tell you."

A voice in my head was saying to me: "Why now? Why? Not
now!" I knew Pogo, and what he thought about it wasn't going to
be any different depending on when I told him. Except that it was
better to tell him before he went into Wesley's house and had more
to drink, which I knew he would do. If it was going to be that day at
all—and the days were numbered, the window of opportunity for
choice, as people liked to call it, would soon close. "So shut up," I
told the voice in my head. "Shut. Up."

I put my arm through Pogo's. "Can we sit down a minute?"

"Sure. I'll finish my cigarette. No smoking in their house now."

"Because of Clementine."

He nodded, took a deep drag, flicked the ash away toward a green
patch of lawn next to the cobblestones. "Here," he said, and we sat
on a step in front of a stranger's house.

"I have to tell you something," I said.

He looked at me with dark suspicion, like I was going to say I'd
cheated on him. "Spit it out," he said.

I hesitated, bit my lip. Now he was really glaring at me. "Say it," he
ordered, smoking furiously.

"I'm pregnant."

He tilted his head back and blew a stream of smoke into the air
and kept staring at it while it dissipated. When he looked down at
me again, he was composed. He patted me on the knee this time.
"Don't worry," he said. "It'll be fine." He put his arm around me and
held me close. I started to cry, quietly.

"No tears, no tears. Didn't I say it'll be fine?"

189

"How will it be fine?" I said.

"You can talk to Ann," he said. "Ann can help you. I'll tell her to call you."

"Ann?" Ann was Pogo's old girlfriend, the one before the one before me. They were still friends. "But I don't know if I want to tell her," I said. "I just now told you."

"Don't worry. You can tell her." He kept patting my knee like he didn't know what else would work. "Everything'll be fine. She'll tell you what to do. She's been through it."

I didn't want to think about the one thing he meant by that.

"How many months?" he finally asked.

"Two. Almost."

"There's time." And he appeared to do some mental calculation. "Are you sure it's mine?"

"Asshole." I punched him hard in the arm. We'd been dating for a year.

He raised his arms to his face, as if to ward off blows. "Violence. Hormones. Hysteria setting in."

"Asshole," I said again. And I buried my face in his chest. He stroked my hair and crushed his cigarette out on the step next to us.

In a minute, he stopped stroking my hair. "Ready to go?" he said.

I lifted my head. He took my purse and rummaged through it until he found a compact mirror. He handed me the mirror. I dabbed at my runny mascara with a tissue. I stood and began to walk back up the hill, the way we came.

"Where are you going?" he said.

Back to the car was where I was going.

"Come on, they're waiting for us," he said.

Of course he still wanted to go. "Don't we need to talk about this?"

"What do you think I should say about it?" said Pogo.

"Well, it *is* your baby, too."

"It's not a baby. It's an amoeba," said Pogo. "It's not a baby until it comes out."

"It's your amoeba," I said. I wanted to say: Why was it different for us than for Cheever and Natasha? We'd known each other longer.

Finally, I did say it.

"We know each other," said Pogo. "That's exactly right. So we know what cloth we're cut from. Don't we?"

I couldn't argue. That may have been the smartest thing I'd ever heard him say. I didn't answer. I just nodded my head. He put his arm around my shoulders, and we walked on down the hill.

Wesley and Kim lived in a row house near Dumbarton Oaks. Wesley's father built golf courses for a living. I don't think Wesley did anything at all. The room where they invited us to sit was called the "parlor." It was formal and full of antiques. There were coasters with green felt on the bottom and pictures of horses and riders in pinks on the top. I don't know why I always noticed coasters. Wesley and Kim were dressed casually, and all of us seemed out of place, as if at any moment a docent would appear to take us on a guided tour of the house and its furnishings. But Wesley and Kim weren't out of place.

Wesley sat down in a wing chair, one leg crossed over the other knee. With a cocktail fork, he prodded a pebble that was lodged in the sole of his loafer.

"There's not a single comfortable chair in this house," he said.

"He's right," said Kim. "The reason these chairs have lasted so long is that no one wants to sit on them."

I sat with Pogo on the loveseat, which was covered in tight green silk and as hard as a church pew. Baby Clementine had just awakened from her nap when we arrived, or maybe we woke her with the door chime. At first she was screaming, but in a little while she was only whimpering, and that only when she caught her mother watching. The screaming was enhanced by an alarming gurgling sound that reminded me of a horror movie in which aliens slit the throats of their victims, whose screams emerge through the bubbling up of blood.

Clementine was almost a year old. She wasn't so much a baby anymore, in my way of thinking. She could stand while grabbing onto things, like the leg of an end table or the arm of a chair, and she'd take a few wobbly steps before sitting back hard on her well-padded bottom. She was comical to watch. She'd let go for a moment, hold her arms out and sway like a drunk who'd risen from a seat in a restaurant after a long meal and was first hit with the full impact of how much she'd had to drink. She'd take a hazardous and misdirected step, wavering all too near the corner of the coffee table for anyone's comfort.

Kim was braced and alert, ready to lunge for Clementine if she should tip toward that sharp corner. Once, she even rose out of her chair partway, but Clementine fell in the other direction instead, away from the table and back on her behind. Kim's whole body exhaled as she sat down again, launch aborted, leaned back and crossed her arms. Until the next time. I understood in that moment, seeing Kim gradually inch toward the edge of her seat yet again, that if you were the mother, you were always waiting for the next time.

I also knew then that I wasn't ready.

$$\Rightarrow$$

If the college breaks had been different by only a few days, the presence of my children might have stopped me. I could list all the usual excuses if I wanted. I had as many excuses as had ever been conceived, and I had no excuse.

When I went to see Pogo the third time, he greeted me in his bathrobe. Flashback to his bathrobe days of yore: lounging in his terry robe, the one with a cigarette burn in the collar, with a large pizza box on his lap and a large hangover.

"There isn't much actual work associated with this work trip, is there?" I said.

He handed me the ice bucket. "Do you mind?" he said. "I don't want to walk down the hall like this." By which I thought he meant the bathrobe, until he pointed to where the silky fabric lifted around his hard-on.

I picked up a corner of his robe. "Peekaboo," I said.

"What about you?" Pogo said. "Don't you work?"

"I take in sewing," I said. I put down the ice bucket. He hooked his fingers through my belt loops and pulled me toward him. I untied his robe. His dick stuck out like a hat rack for a hydrocephalic midget.

I was doing something I couldn't explain even to myself. "I'm here looking for a venue for my daughter's college graduation party," I said. It was a bad joke. I looked away from his dick, anywhere else, the brass table lamp. I switched it on.

"Your daughter," he said.

"Yes."

This was, I suppose, the definition of an uncomfortable silence. Did he not know I had children?

Even if I hadn't considered the so-called "amoeba" a person at eight weeks, I thought of it, against my will, as a baby. I'd held in my mind the generic image of what might have been: A blue-eyed, golden-haired infant in a Pampers commercial—nothing like me or Pogo. Once I did have children, I spent less time thinking about what I'd done. I tried to convince myself that I was guilty only of bad judgment and youthful naiveté. But it was always there, the not-boy not-girl not-baby, as if my mind had gone ahead and given birth to it. I could still see it. The ghost child I never had.

It had been just about the worst thing I could have imagined. Until the even worse thing happened. Pogo didn't know that my sister had died, to say nothing of the way she'd died. In her behavior, Donna had been the model child I never could be. Our parents, blind, like any parents, had always said she never gave them any trouble; they didn't comment on that final trouble. If only I'd understood sooner.

My sister's body had been fixed up so we could see her one last time in the hospital. She was under a blanket, it was tucked all around her, up to her neck. But I could see her chin, her head, which they'd bandaged, her face, which they'd tried their best to clean up. Her eyes were closed. One hand was uncovered, resting on the blanket, the blue cast of her skin on white. I stood at the end of her bed, and while my parents held her hands and gazed at her still, battered face, I held onto her foot through the blanket. It felt like clay. For years after, I couldn't look at my children in bed, their feet shifting and wriggling underneath their blankets, and not think of my sister.

"YES," I SAID. "My daughter." I reached into my purse to pull out my phone and show him a photo, but changed my mind.

"Were you surprised to hear from me?" he said.

"Yes," I said. He hadn't asked me that when he saw me in March or in April.

He pulled at my pants. "Wait—there's a hook," I said.

"No waiting," he said.

He lifted my shirt over my head and rubbed his cheek against my breast. It was scratchy in a good way. He maneuvered me backward.

"Pogo," I said. I put my legs around his neck, drawing him in and trapping him. "Porter. Have you been tested?"

"Many times," he said.

"You know what I mean," I said.

"Yes, I'm healthy," he said. "Except for the pollen whenever I come back here." He fake-sneezed into my belly. "Now *'scuse me while I kiss the sky*." And he put his head down between my legs, but I put a foot on his shoulder and stopped him.

"Whenever?" I said. "How many times have you been back?"

"A few times a year, for work."

I scooted away from him and sat up, leaned against the padded headboard.

"Come back, you're all wet," he said.

"Stop looking at me," I said. I pulled a pillow onto my lap. He grabbed my ankles and yanked them.

"You lied," I said.

He attempted to pry my legs apart and then climbed over them, straddling me instead.

"Why now?" I said. "Answer me."

He sighed and stopped what he was doing and rolled onto his back. "I thought of you every single time I was here," he said. "I thought of calling or emailing. Summoning you with smoke signals."

"And you didn't."

"Right."

I put my hand on his cheek and turned it, forced him to look at me. I wanted to kiss him, even though I was angry. Because I was angry.

"I didn't want," he started. "I didn't want us to meet for coffee, for lunch, and I'd say how are the kids? How's the house? Are you still working? And you'd say, the kids are good, and dressing on the side please, and my life is a treasure of happiness and we're remodeling the basement."

"What's wrong with that?" I said. "That's chat. It's the beginning of talk. There could be real talk."

"That's not the point," he said.

"Okay," I said.

"Stop talking," he said.

I stopped.

I was on my side, and he brought his face close to mine. I noticed the scar on his forehead, tried to think what it reminded me of. He put his fingers inside me and moved them around and he took my hand and put it on his cock, which was hard and staying that way.

And then something inside the pillow pricked at my cheek. I started up. "Feathers," I said.

"Only the best for you," said Pogo.

"It stabbed me," I said. "Stop."

"Stop?" he said.

I squirmed away from him. "I have to go."

"What?" He had his cock in his hand. "I have a rubber," he said.

"It's not that." I got out of bed and went to the bathroom and locked the door. He rattled the doorknob.

"What the hell?" he said.

I scalded myself the best I could with hot water using the hotel's white washcloth. I'd shower at home. "I have to go," I said again.

"But where? When are you coming back?"

I was pulling on my pants and he was putting on his robe, as if he meant to follow me. "I'm not sure," I said. "I forgot about something."

I ran down the hall, but my footsteps made no sound on the carpet. I looked behind me at the last minute, before I got on the elevator, and he was standing outside his room staring after me. I didn't turn to salt.

WHEN I GOT home, I went to the kitchen window, but I didn't see the hawk. And then I found it, in one of the oak trees that grew in my yard. It was higher up, that's why I hadn't spotted it at first. I went for the binoculars. Downy feathers floated around the hawk's head. Flesh hung from its beak. I saw the pastel gray head of a mourning dove drooping in the grip of the hawk's talons. That's why the hawk was perched so low before; it was after the ground-nesting doves. While I watched, it dropped the dove and flew off, as if it had had enough.

➔

When Pogo picked me up from the clinic, he'd brought me a large stuffed bear, a gift you might buy for a new baby. I wanted to hide from its goofy stupid grin, its big cheap satin bow. He took me to a nice restaurant for lunch, as if that emptying out had made me hungry. He ordered me a screwdriver, even though I wasn't supposed to drink. To Pogo, it was always a good idea to buy someone a drink; that was something I used to like about him. He drank it instead, and we drove to his place, where he kissed me and put a hand inside my shirt and wanted to know when I might feel like having sex.

Never, I told him.

And never stayed never for long enough that we broke up. I knew it was better. I saw myself in a strangely Victorian light in those days. Damaged.

➔

The last time I went to see him at the hotel, Pogo put a finger to my lips when I tried to speak. He was in a hurry. He wasn't taking a chance that I'd leave again. I told myself I'd gone back to make sure that I wouldn't regret *not* going.

"I don't want to lose it this time," he said, in my ear, his face in my hair.

I turned my head enough to see him behind me. And I remembered how he'd brought me to the bleachers and tried to persuade me back then, when we'd just started dating and I was free to do as I pleased. It was dark, but he had a flashlight and a blanket and found a clean place in the grass, with no beer cans or cigarette butts, and he'd spread out the blanket and we kissed and he took off my shirt and my bra. And I said no.

"What do you mean, 'no'?" he said, now. "Goddammit." He rolled off of me onto his back. "What are we here for?"

"I'm sorry," I said. "Can't we both be sorry?" Because right then I felt sorry about everything, about the way I'd lived, about being foolish enough to believe that the only change that mattered could fit inside a pamphlet.

He stroked himself and cursed. "I was ready," he said.

I let my cheek sink into the slippery silk duvet, grabbed at the fabric with my fingers, as if it were dear life.

ACKNOWLEDGMENTS

This book could not have come about without the support of more people than I can name, and yet I will try. Endless gratitude:

To Afonso Albergaria and his students at the Young Women's Leadership School of East Harlem, who planted the seed for this book when they told me they wanted to read more about the girl in "Driver's Education."

To Daniel Menaker, for his unflagging faith in my talents, his fine editorial judgment, and his indispensable sense of humor. To David McCormick, Bridget McCarthy, and Emma Borges-Scott at Mc-Cormick Literary for their support.

To my editor, Mike Levine, for saying that he loved the book right away, and to everyone at Northwestern University Press who has had a hand in bringing this book to life, including Henry Carrigan, Nathan MacBrien, Greta Bennion, and Marianne Jankowski.

To Kathy Daneman, for her energy, creativity, and patience.

To all of the early teachers who encouraged me in my writing, and therefore are at least partly to blame for my persistence, especially Wesley Walker and Joyce Kornblatt.

To Kermit Moyer, my mentor and teacher, my longtime careful reader, and my friend; and to all of the good people from my years in The American University's M.F.A. program.

To my friends and colleagues who have been generous with their advice, encouragement, and critical insights, and, when called for, shoulders to lean on and martinis: Carolyn Parkhurst, Leslie

Pietrzyk, Amy Stolls, Susan Coll, Dylan Landis, Joel Hoffman, Mary Morris, Percival Everett, Bill Goldstein, Robert Markowitz, Cheryl Tan, and Blake Bailey.

To the D.C. Women Writers, for the essential community.

To the journal editors who published earlier versions of some of these stories: Andrew Altschul, David Daley, Paula Deitz, Marc Drew, Stephen Elliott, W. Ralph Eubanks, Jessy Goodman, Ellen Hathaway, Ron Koury, Margot Livesey, Susan Merrell, Richard Peabody, Ladette Randolph, Marisa Siegel, and Peter Stitt.

To the dedicated teachers who invited me into their classrooms and introduced my stories to their students, and to the Pen/Faulkner Foundation, *The Hudson Review*, and CUNY/College Now for making those inspiring exchanges possible.

To The MacDowell Colony, the Corporation of Yaddo, The Studios of Key West, VCCA, the Sewanee Writers' Conference, the Arts & Humanities Council of Montgomery County, and the Key West Literary Seminar for the crucial and generous support, which always seemed to come at the moment I needed it most.

To Juliet Nieto, for being my right hand, and to Mary O., for helping me keep my head.

To my parents, Max and Susan, for their consistently biased and uncritical praise, for fostering my love of reading, and for teaching me about storytelling by raising me on stories they didn't want repeated—those are the best stories of all. To Susie, because she understands, and to Frank, for his pep talks—even though he won't see this, his influence is felt. To my husband Bill for his unwavering support and his perpetual optimism on my behalf, and for so much that is intangible. To my sons, David and Eric, for reading my stories surreptitiously and laughing in the right places, and in a strange turn of the tables, being proud of my accomplishments. You all are more important to me than any fiction.

➜

Some of these stories were originally published in slightly different form in the following venues:

"Self Report," *Ploughshares*

"Bad Side In," *The Southampton Review*

"Transfigured Night," *Virginia Quarterly Review*

"Jump," *Gargoyle Magazine*

"Driver's Education," originally published in *The Hudson Review*, republished in *Writes of Passage: Coming-of-Age Stories and Memoirs from "The Hudson Review"* (Chicago: Ivan R. Dee, 2008).

"You May See a Stranger," *The Gettysburg Review*

"Just Sex," *Weekly Rumpus*

"Dubrovnik 1989," *Five Chapters*